CUPID
COMPUTER

❧ ❧

CUPID
COMPUTER

by
Margie Milcsik

Aladdin Books
Macmillan Publishing Company   New York
Maxwell Macmillan Canada   Toronto
Maxwell Macmillan International
New York   Oxford   Singapore   Sydney

First Aladdin Books edition 1992
Copyright © 1981 by Margie Milcsik

Aladdin Books   Maxwell Macmillan Canada, Inc.
Macmillan Publishing Company   1200 Eglinton Avenue East
866 Third Avenue   Suite 200
New York, NY 10022   Don Mills, Ontario M3C 3N1

Macmillan Publishing Company is part of the Maxwell Communication
Group of Companies.

Printed in the United States of America
10 9 8 7 6 5 4 3 2 1

Library of Congress Cataloging-in-Publication Data
Milcsik, Margie.
Cupid computer / by Margie Milcsik. — 1st Aladdin Books ed.
        p.   cm.
Summary: Driven by teenage insecurities, competitiveness, and that
yearning for a "first" boyfriend, Toni tries to outwit a computer to
land a date for her school's Valentine's Day dance.
ISBN 0-689-71569-2
I. Title.
[PZ7.M5937Cu 1992]
[Fic]—dc20   91-46152

Thanks, St. Jude

CONTENTS

This is probably the worst night of my whole entire life. Wait . . . I take that back. It isn't "probably" the worst. It is definitely the worst.

I know my mother says I always exaggerate and that I'm overly dramatic—but believe me—this is without a doubt the most horrible, the most humiliating, the most depressing—well, it's the grossest night of my whole life.

It's revolting! Only twelve and already I've experienced the pits of human emotion, the depths of darkest despair. My life is practically over. Over! Toni Moretti washed up before I ever see the golden age of thirteen. A has-been in the prime of life.

The only thing left for me now is the convent. Just a life of penance and prayer. Or suffering and hard work. Typical. God won't even have mercy on me as a nun. Forget *The Sound of Music*. With my luck, I'll probably be shipped off to Africa to heal the lepers.

That's what they did to Audrey Hepburn in *The Nun's Story*. Only I won't have some movie director to yell "cut—print." I'll be stuck in some jungle for real. Sweaty, sick, cannibal bait with a million mosquito bites all over my wretched eighty-five-pound body. My skinny little nun knees buckled from prayer. My brain delirious with fever and . . .

What am I doing! Forget Africa. I'm suffering enough right here. Maybe I should give St. Anthony another try. You'd think my undying faith in him would count for something. Especially at this point. Patron saint of lost causes. Hah! How much more hopelessness does he need?

7:03 . . . only fifty-seven minutes until the beginning of the end. Well, I guess I better get ready. Ready for what I don't know. Except of course, if you count total and complete humiliation.

What a lost cause. Did you hear that, St. Anthony? I said, "lost cause." Where are you when I need you?

And where were you when I needed you in the first place?

Chapter 1

THANK YOU, IBM

ঽ ঙ

I guess St. Anthony doesn't hang around junior high schools. At least he doesn't hang around mine, because that's where the whole mess started a week ago. Either he flew south for the winter, or he was goofing off in the divine guidance department. All I know is that he sure didn't send me any signals of foreboding doom.

It was Thursday, during Miss Kramer's Sewing 1 class. I hate Sewing 1. I'd hate Sewing 2, 3, or anything else that had to do with needles and thread. I also hate Miss Kramer. She's the sarcastic type. The kind that's real smug and smiles when she says, "fine," even though she really means, "it stinks."

She gets plenty of opportunity to use her sarcastic remarks with me, too. Mainly because I can't sew. According to her, Toni Moretti is the only girl in five years to flunk aprons. That's because I sewed the hem to the waistband and when I ripped out the stitches, I ripped the material too.

My father said not to worry about it because Italians cook better than they sew. I wanted to tell Miss Kramer to wait until Spaghetti Sauce 1, but I thought I'd better not press my luck before I mastered the Simplicity blouse stage. (Which should be in about twenty years, if I ever figure out how to thread that dumb bobbin.)

However, last Thursday, for once in my life, I didn't hate Sewing 1. I didn't hate it because I didn't have it. Class was just beginning when I was mercifully saved by the intercom. Mr. Simmons, our seventh-grade advisor, announced over the loudspeaker that an assembly was scheduled for the seventh grade and everyone had to attend.

This didn't exactly thrill Miss Kramer. She's sort of anti-assembly. Especially when it interrupts her class. Now I, unlike Miss Kramer, am very pro-assembly. Especially when it interrupts her class. Even Kate and Brenda—even they agree with me. And they're already on to pleated skirts. They know how to sew, and they still hate Miss Kramer. Of course, when you're friends like the three of us were, you agree on everything. You stick together. Through anything—and I do mean anything. Including a Home Ec. teacher like you know who.

But back to assemblies. One thing I really like about them is that before things settle down, you get a chance to talk without threat of detention. Also, if you're careful, you can chew gum with-

out some teacher making you spit it ou
I like assemblies because they're in th
which is one of my absolute favorite
entire school.

Two months ago, that's where I
guess you could call my stage debut. Our sen
put on the musical, *Once Upon a Mattress*, and I
was chosen to play Princess Winnifred. The
teacher who directed the play told my parents that
I was a natural-born actress. I always told my
mother that watching old movies on TV wasn't a
waste of time. And my sister said memorizing every
"I Love Lucy" episode by heart was dumb. That's
how much she knows. There was a lot of Lucy in
Winnifred.

Anyway, everybody said my performance was
really good. Especially when I sang my "Swamps
of Home" number. One night I even got five curtain calls. When I heard that applause, that's when I
knew I was destined for a life in the theater. Acting was in my blood. *That* I told Miss Kramer. She
told me she knew it wasn't sewing. Like I said, she's
the sarcastic type.

I'm getting off the track. Anyway, Miss Kramer
is nothing compared to what all started last week.

It didn't seem any different from other assemblies. Kate, Brenda and I walked down one of the
aisles in the auditorium, and the three of us sat
down in the front row. I put my books under the

and passed out the Juicy Fruit, two sticks for each of us. I didn't really want to sit so close to the stage because I'd have to be extra careful with my chews, and with two sticks in your mouth you have some big chews. But Brenda insisted. She wanted to get a good view of Mr. Simmons, but didn't want him to see her wearing glasses.

She thinks he's a hunk, which means she thinks he's macho, which means she's crazy about him. Now if he looked like Cary Grant—or better yet, Clark Gable—I could understand what she sees in him. But Mr. Simmons? I guess he's O.K. if you like hair, but he's a far cry from Rhett Butler.

I only had a few good chomps on the Juicy Fruit when onto the stage walked the hunk . . . I mean Mr. Simmons. He tapped the microphone, said the usual "testing, one, two, three," and then asked for attention. Everyone stopped talking, and I pushed the gum to the corner of my mouth and tried to remember not to chew. I didn't want to have to spit out a wad of Juicy Fruit in front of three hundred kids. Brenda squinted up at the stage and grabbed Kate's wrist sighing, "What a you-know-what."

I honestly don't know what she sees in him. Someone with hair even on his knuckles is nothing to sigh over in my book. Now, if you wanted to talk sighing, besides Clark Gable that is, I'd say talk Kevin McEvoy. He's our class president, and he was up on stage too. So were the other class officers, but who could bother with them when you could look at Kevin.

Kevin is cute. I mean CUTE. His hair is brown, a little lighter than mine and, of course, shorter. It sort of curls over his ears and hugs the back of his neck. He has an absolutely terrific smile and, well —just take my word for it. He's cute. I sit across from him in history class, so believe me, I can vouch for his cuteness.

I caught myself doing a Brenda sigh just as Mr. Simmons said something about a Valentine's Dance.

". . . and so, we are going to try something special this year. It's a little different, and I think it should be a lot of fun for everyone."

I slouched in my seat. If it was a dance, "everyone" did not include me. Not because I can't dance. It's just that the male population in our school doesn't exactly consider me a *femme fatale*. Toni Moretti may be Italian, but that's where the similarity between me and Sophia Loren begins and ends. If you know what I mean. All the boys do anyway. I don't have enough "femme" for them to be "fatale" over.

As Mr. Simmons' voice echoed in the auditorium, I tried to remember what my mother is always telling me. My day will come. Sure. But by that time, I'll probably be too old to enjoy it.

Brenda was still squinting and sighing when I

heard Mr. Simmons say something about a computer.

". . . It's what your student council has called a computer dance. A sort of "Cupid Computer." And everyone in the school can participate. All you will have to do is answer this questionnaire," he said, holding up a blue paper. "Then our programmed Cupid will scientifically match you, based on likes and dislikes, with a dream date to the Valentine's Dance."

I sat up and nudged Kate who nudged Brenda. This computer idea didn't sound too bad. Not bad at all. In fact, it sounded pretty good. If Mother Nature wasn't going to cooperate with my social life—then science could take over. How could a computer tell the difference between me and Sophia?

"You'll understand more about what I'm saying when you see a copy of the questionnaire, which everyone can pick up in the main lobby today," Mr. Simmons continued as I looked back up at the stage. "Who knows, the valentine of your dreams might be in this auditorium right now, just waiting for our computerized Cupid to bring you together."

By the time Mr. Simmons introduced a man from the computer company, I was sitting on the edge of my seat and had accidentally swallowed my gum.

I sat with a lump of Juicy Fruit in my throat as I listened to the computer man explain all about the hows, whats, do's and don'ts concerning the questionnaire.

"Doesn't this sound great?" whispered Kate.

"Yeah, and easy," I whispered back as the man talked. "And one of the best parts is that we'll all get to go to the dance together. You, Brenda and me—the three of us with boyfriends. Dates! Boy, I never thought I'd be saying this, but isn't science wonderful?"

It had to be wonderful if it was going to get the three of us boyfriends. None of us—Kate, Brenda or me—had ever gone to a dance before. With a boy that is. I've never even been to a boy-girl party. Well, not since the fourth grade, and I don't think that really counts.

I was beginning to give up hope of ever having a boyfriend. I thought I'd be the last girl on earth to get a date. Especially since last December when Kate was asked to a Christmas Dance by a boy who goes to another school. She didn't go though. Luckily, the boy got the flu.

I really don't mean luckily. What I mean is . . . well . . . it was just that Brenda and I weren't asked by anybody and . . . well, this time it will be different because we'll all get to go together.

After the computer man instructed us not to

fold, spindle or mutilate our questionnaires, Mr. Simmons introduced the class officers and then asked Kevin to say a few words.

Talk about dream dates. This definitely called for a Brenda-style Mr. Simmons sigh. Kevin isn't quite the Clark Gable—*Gone With The Wind* type either, but as I said before, for a thirteen-year-old, he's right up there.

"Everyone will get their results in homeroom on this coming Monday, the tenth," he said stepping up to the microphone as Mr. Simmons took a seat again on the stage. "I think that will give everyone plenty of time to get to know their computer match before the dance next week. That is of course, unless the computer happens to match you with someone you already know."

Someone I already knew? Hmmm. While Kevin continued talking, my mind shifted into high gear. I felt the little wheels in my head spinning and clicking. One of my "I Love Lucy" plans was cooking up there.

All I remembered about what Kevin said was that he hoped the dance was a success. That made two of us I thought, applauding as he finished speaking.

Mr. Simmons dismissed us for our next class, and I picked up my books from beneath the seat and waited to file out into the aisle. As Kate stepped out from our row, I looked back at the stage to see Kevin walk behind the curtain.

A computer dance.

Yes, I thought. This could definitely be a success.

Who said it's not nice to fool Mother Nature?

Chapter 2

NUMBER EIGHT

୬ ୧

What's the point of having an assembly—one that could change your whole life—when you can't even talk about it in the next class? Not even to one of your best friends. I ask you, where's the justice in this world?

I thought I was going to die in Science. (And I was the one who said it was wonderful?) Talking is quote not tolerated unquote. Usually I don't mind that rule. Well, I do mind it a little—but after an assembly like the one we had just had, who wouldn't?

And to make matters worse, Mr. Hargrove has to be the most boring teacher in the whole school. Nice, but boring. He is sort of interesting to look at though. Not interesting the way Brenda thinks Mr. Simmons is interesting, but interesting. Mr. Hargrove kind of looks like a turtle. Especially when he gives notes. Then his head rocks back and forth and his eyes bulge. But it's really only good for five or ten minutes of note-taking entertainment. And that's on one of his good days. Usually after a few head bobs, it's all downhill.

Last Thursday was not one of his "good" days. It wasn't even one of his "bad" days. It was the pits. The absolute, quiet, boring, downhill pits. Kate and I sat right next to each other, and we couldn't even sneak one whisper about the computer, the dance, nothing.

Finally, after forty-five minutes of agonizing enforced silence, the bell rang. Kate and I grabbed our books and rushed out of the science lab and ran down the hall. We probably would have trampled anyone in our path to get to the gym to meet Brenda. Next to assemblies, gym is the best time to get in some serious talking. And since Brenda was picking up questionnaires for all of us during passing, we would really have some good stuff to talk about.

"Well, let's see those things already," said Kate as the three of us pushed open the gym doors and ran to our lockers.

"I only had a chance to look at a few of the questions," said Brenda handing one to each of us, "but the whole thing looks fantastic. It asks everything," she said taking off her glasses and putting them in her bag, which hung on the locker hook.

I sat down on the bench and put the questionnaire on my lap, reading as I dialed the locker combination.

"Look at number fourteen . . . and number twelve," said Kate as she pulled up her sweat socks. "Right here," she said, pointing on my questionnaire. "Where you like to go, what you like to do, and—"

"And what you want your computer match to look like. Don't forget that one," said Brenda. "Gee, I wonder who I'll be matched with. Do you think there's any boy in school who looks like Mr. Simmons?"

Mr. Simmons. Well, Brenda could think about getting matched with someone like him if she wanted to. (Only I doubt if any boy our age has that much hair. Even on his head.) I had my own idea about who I wanted the computer to match me with.

I opened my locker and got a whiff of that old stale Fritos corn chip smell. I still can't figure out why gym stuff always smells like Fritos, but it does. I dumped my books, unzipped my jeans, and was kicking off my shoes when a voice yelled over from the row of lockers behind ours.

It was Bobbi Weston.

"Hey you guys . . . get a load of number eight. The one about physical description," she called to no one in particular. "Definitely my kind of question, huh?"

It figured that that would be the one to get her all hot and bothered. Bobbi Weston was not exactly lacking in the physical description department. She never let anyone forget it either. As if they could.

I tried to get her body out of my mind and get into my gym suit before Mrs. Cassidy started blowing her whistle for class. Believe me, it's not easy to ignore someone talking about what a great body she has when you're stuck undressing your own, which rates semi-fair. If I didn't know better, I'd swear Bobbi stuffed her bra with sweat socks. Unfortunately, I do know better. I saw her once in the shower. She's for real. Really for real.

"Hey, Toni . . . read number eight yet?" Bobbi asked again as she passed by my locker.

Boy that girl has good posture . . . or something.

"Yeah, I read number eight," I said hanging my pullover sweater on the locker hook as I tried to stand up straighter.

"So? . . . What do you think I should answer for question number eight? Really. Be honest. I mean, wouldn't you describe my physical build as above average?"

Above average, I thought. Oh brother.

"Not that I'm really above average or anything, but compared to others . . . well, you know. I guess you're going to have to answer petite, huh? You always look 'petite'," she said sitting down and folding her arms around her knees. "Especially up on stage. Like when you were in that play."

I could tell what was coming. She'd only said it about two million times. Ever since she auditioned for that play and didn't get the part of Winnifred, she had been blabbing to everyone that it was because she was "too sexy." I was the only girl who "fit" the character—and the costume. "Typecasting" she called it.

"Anyway," said Bobbi watching me step into my gym suit, "that's what I figured. So . . . it sounds like you're pretty excited about this computer dance thing. I heard the three of you talking about it when you came in."

She's an eavesdropper, too.

"Yeah, well, I think it's a good idea," I said. "Don't you?"

"Hmmmm? I guess," she said, twirling her blonde hair around her fingers. "Especially for someone who's never gone steady or even dated."

Zinger number two.

"But, I don't know. Do you think that computer will really work? I mean . . . for you?"

"For me? Bobbi, what do you mean, 'for me'? It's science. Didn't you hear that man from the

[18]

computer company? It's foolproof. All you have to do is answer the questions on the sheet. How can it not work?"

I knew as soon as I said it that that was the wrong thing to ask. Bobbi had that know-it-all look on her face and was staring at me as I snapped my gym suit.

"Well, if you really want me to tell you, Toni . . . Hey—what are you wearing? It doesn't look like a bra. Toni Moretti, don't tell me you don't wear a bra!"

Zinger number three. Why did that girl have to notice everything?

"Of course I wear a bra, Bobbi," I said snapping faster while she kept smiling. "It's just that sometimes, well, sometimes I wear this. It's called a camisole . . . that's French, in case you didn't know."

Actually I started wearing my sister Jeannie's camisole not because it's French, but because I couldn't stand wearing that bra. Not that I'd ever tell Bobbi that, but at least the camisole is comfortable. And, it's not form-fitting either, which is good for me since there isn't much form to fit. Besides, all the movie stars in the 1930s wore them. Bobbi obviously never saw Bette Davis in her underwear.

Luckily I was spared any more of her dumb conversation because Mrs. Cassidy was blowing her final whistle for roll call.

I snapped the last snap on my gym suit, pulled up my socks, and made a quick exit. I left Bobbi with that know-it-all smile on her face and ran into the gym to find Brenda and Kate.

After Mrs. Cassidy took attendance and gave assignments, we got into groups to practice our gymnastics. My group was working on the mats, which I like a lot better than the balance beam or parallel bars.

This marking period, besides all the cartwheels and rolls, we also have to do something like a dance routine. That was one thing I could handle. Fortunately, not only is acting in my blood, but dancing is in my feet. In fact, this is the only time of the year I can manage an A in phys. ed. Dancing is about as athletic as I get. Luckily with the computer dance, I was beginning to believe that I'd finally do some dancing in something other than a gym suit. Whoever designed those things should be shot. Didn't they ever read *Seventeen?*

The gym was its usual noisy place with lots of sneakers squeaking and springboards bouncing. But that day, adding to the decibel level were the conversations every girl, the three of us included, was having about the computer dance.

"What are you going to put down for number twelve?" Brenda asked as she bent down into a tripod position and I got ready to spot her head-stand.

Kate took out the questionnaire she had stuffed in her pocket and started to read off all the choices. "O.K., let's see . . . number twelve: What activities are you interested in?: (a) tennis (b) baseball (c) swimming (d) skiing (e) music (f) dancing (g) reading (h) crafts."

"I think I'm going to check them all," said Brenda, her legs wobbling above her blonde head. "Cover all bases. I don't want to get too picky. No sense making it too tough for the computer to find me a match."

"Yeah, smart, only you better not check reading," I said. "The computer could match you with John Carney."

"EEEEEeeeeeeeeeych!" she screamed toppling over onto me. "Creepy Carney? That bookworm?"

I laughed as we helped each other up from the mat. "Why? What's wrong? I thought you and John Carney were the perfect couple. You both like to read and . . ."

"Perfect couple. Oh, thanks, Toni. Ha. Ha. Very funny."

"Well, you know, you two, with a computer anything is possible," said Kate doing a cartwheel in front of us. "The more things you have in common with somebody, the more chance there is of being matched. It's the way you said, if your answer is 'reading,' and some boy answers the same thing, well, the computer will probably match you. That's how computers work. The more alike two people are, the more chance there is that you'll be matched."

That was how computers worked? Maybe that was what Bobbi tried to tell me in the locker room. If what boys thought was important wasn't what I had, then what chance was there for me? I began wondering if that dream date business wasn't such a sure thing after all.

"Hey, listen Brenda. Kate's right," I said. "We're going to have to be careful how we answer those questionnaires."

"Well, let's be careful then," said Brenda. "Really careful. I don't want anything to mess up my chances of going to the Valentine's Dance. At least you were asked to a dance once already, Kate, but I might never get an opportunity like this again. . . . But, hey," she said standing up, "Really, isn't this going to be great? I mean, the three of us going to our first dance together. Boy, I hope I'm matched with somebody I like."

"Me too," agreed Kate as we lined up in front of a mat where everyone was doing forward rolls. "I just hope that computer knows who I want to be matched with, because I sure don't."

"You don't?" I said thinking about the morning assembly. "Well, I know who I want to be matched with."

"And who is that, Toni?" said Bobbi Weston sneaking up behind us.

The big eavesdropper again. Why was that girl always around at the wrong time? I wanted to tell her to leave us alone and mind her own business, but I didn't. Which was a mistake. A big mistake, because then she told me all over again not to count on a date for the computer dance.

"And just why shouldn't Toni count on a date," asked Brenda confidently.

"Why not?" said Bobbi. "I can't believe you're standing there asking me that. . . . Come on, Brenda, do I really have to tell you?" she said throwing her shoulders back. "Everyone knows how all the really neat, cute, 'mature' boys will answer those questionnaires. Especially the part where they describe what they want their dream dates to look like."

"Well, I don't," said Kate turning around. "What are you talking about, Bobbi?"

"Look, take it from me. I know what boys like and . . . well . . . let's just say," she said staring at me, "that the boys won't be checking 'petite' on those questionnaires when it comes to number eight. That might leave some of you girls without dates for the dance."

Well, there went another dance down the drain,

I thought as I felt Bobbi's eyes looking right through me. That was one morning when I should have suffered through wearing that uncomfortable padded bra instead of a camisole. Bette Davis or not.

"Oh, Bobbi, that's ridiculous," said Kate coming to my defense. "Don't pay any attention to her, Toni. Number eight isn't the only question. There are plenty of other questions on that sheet that will match us with someone we like—and who likes us, too. Besides, Bobbi, I don't think that question or any other has anything to do with what you're talking about. It's ridiculous."

"You think it's ridiculous, Kate Donnelly? Fine. You'll see," she said tossing her hair back. "I'm just warning you, that's all."

"Well, gee, thanks so much for the warning," Kate said calmly. "But I think the three of us can manage being matched without your help. C'mon, Brenda, Toni. We've wasted enough time. Let's do some forward rolls. On another mat."

"O.K., go ahead," Bobbi called as Kate and Brenda walked over to the other side of the gym. "But, Toni," she said before I joined them, "remember, those questionnaires work two ways. As I said, it's not just what you like or don't like. It's what the boy likes, too. He's also filling out one of those things, you know. Remember," she said grabbing my arm, "boys have their own ideas of what makes a girl a dream date. And *that's* how the computer is going to do its matching."

"Oh, and I suppose you think all the boys will want to be matched with you," I said as she let go of my elbow.

"Maybe . . . maybe I'd say it's a good possibility. If you know what I mean."

I looked at Bobbi and then at her 34-B chest that just about popped out of her gym suit. I had a funny feeling I knew exactly what she meant. Unfortunately, I didn't think I could grow breasts overnight.

Zinger number eight.

Chapter 3

STARS

≥ ᴋ

"AAAAAAAAAAAAAAAAAAAaaaaaaaaaaaaah hhhhhhhhhhh."

I slammed the front door, dragged myself into the family room and fell on the couch. I didn't bother to take off my jacket. I kicked off one shoe and stared at the ceiling.

What a day. What a lousy day. How could one day have started off so great and ended up so crummy? I should have known that not having Miss Kramer plus getting a chance to go to a dance all in the same day was too good to be true. And that computer idea sounded so good. Science. Hah! Even that had a catch. Now I knew for sure I'd be old and gray before I ever had a date and a boyfriend. I was going to be the only one, I thought. Brenda and Kate—the whole school would go to that dance—except me. Darn that Bobbi Weston and her 'number eight.' I could have just . . .

"AAAAaaaaaaaaaaaaaaahhhhhhhhhhhhhhhhh."

"Toni? Is that you screaming down there?" my

mother called from the upstairs hallway.

"Yeah, Ma. It's my therapy. I heard it on the 'Hollywood Squares.' I'm screaming to relieve my pent-up emotions. I'm depressed. AAAAAA-aaaaaaahhhhhhhh . . ."

"Well, if you don't stop that screaming immediately, you, my dear daughter, are going to be more depressed than even you can imagine," she said, walking into the room making the same old spanking gesture that she's made ever since I was three years old. Only she's never followed through. Well, almost never. "And why are you lying there still wearing your jacket?"

I slowly covered my eyes with my arm and said, "It's been one of those days, Ma, you know?"

"Yes, I know. We all know," she said sitting in the plaid armchair in the corner of the room. "Didn't you just have 'one of those days' last week?"

My mother has absolutely no sense of the dramatic.

"Ma!" I said sitting up and unzipping my jacket. "This is serious—extremely serious. This is my one and only chance of a lifetime, and I'm going to blow it. It's the turning point. I'm at the crossroads of my existence, and—Ma-a-a. Don't call me Tallulah!"

I could tell she was just dying to say it. My mother always calls me that when she thinks I'm being too dramatic, which she thinks is all the time. Why I remind her of Tallulah Bankhead, though, is beyond me. I saw her once on an old "I Love Lucy" episode, and I'm absolutely nothing like her. Well, maybe a little. I do move my arms around a lot . . . and I talk pretty fast . . . but that's it.

"O.K. then," my mother said as she crossed her legs and tried not to smile. (I hate when she tries not to smile because she knows that I know she's really smiling.) "What is the 'extremely' serious problem that warrants all these theatrics? Again."

Talk about unsympathetic mothers. I bet Tallulah never had to cope with insensitivity like that.

"Ma-a-a, I'm not kidding. This is really serious," I said, standing up and pacing the floor. "The problem is—and actually I think it's all your fault —you and Daddy—for giving me defective genes— The problem is THIS!" I said, pointing both thumbs to my chest. "The problem is my boobs. Or," I said, looking down at myself, "what boobs?"

"Toni!"

"Well, Mom, you asked," I said watching as she gave me one of her "looks."

"What did I tell you about using language like . . ."

"Oh, Ma! Jeannie calls hers that all the time," I said sitting on the carpet. "And . . ."

"And, may I remind you, young lady, your sister is eighteen years old."

Whatever that meant. I wondered if my mother was telling me you didn't call them "that" until you were eighteen years old. I wondered, but I didn't ask. I didn't want to chance anything worse than a look, so I went right to the problem with the computer dance.

I told her how good it sounded until Bobbi Weston explained what boys liked and what I don't have for them to like, which all meant: no match, no date, no nothing. Naturally, my mother thought I was exaggerating the whole thing out of proportion. She didn't understand. That was the problem. I had no proportion.

"Ma, I'm not exaggerating. Look at me. I need help. I'm desperate. Ma, listen," I begged kneeling by her arm chair, "Could you buy me a Mark Eden developer? Please? It isn't that expensive. You can count it towards my next year's Christmas gifts. We can have it delivered air mail—rapid transit . . ."

"Toni, honey," she said laughing.

So much for Mark Eden. And so much for my mother. That's the way she always starts her "no's." Then she went into her "be patient" philosophy about my non-existent you-know-whats and told me not to worry and relax. And of course, she ended up with her old stand-by, "everything will work out fine."

"But Ma . . ."

"No buts. For heaven's sake Toni, you're fine just as you are."

Mothers always say stuff like that. They have to. I think it's in the Mother's Manual or something.

"Well, enough of this," she said getting up from the chair.

Enough of this? My life was falling apart, and my own mother was saying enough of this?

"I've got to get dinner started. Daddy will be home in about an hour, and Jeannie's last class should be over around four-thirty," she said heading for the kitchen. "So, I'll call you in a little while to set the table."

So much for understanding and parental guidance. And dinner! How could she think of food at a time like this?

I didn't know why she was starting dinner so early anyway. My father was still on his diet. He decided last month that a police chief should be fit and trim as an example for the rest of the force. Unfortunately, we all had to starve along with him. The only thing the whole family had been eating for weeks was cottage cheese.

I probably would have died of malnutrition in January if it hadn't been for my grandmother. For the past month the highlight of my life had been lasagna at her house for Sunday dinner. When you think about it, having lasagna as the highlight of your life, even if you're a kid, is pretty depressing.

My whole life was depressed.

I felt another scream coming on, but I suppressed it and turned on the television instead. I had almost forgotten, with everything I had to worry about, that it was time for my favorite soap opera.

Today was going to be a good day, too. Head nurse Renee Howard was going to poison Dr. Parker, resident rat at Mercy General, with some cream puffs. Actually, she had made them the Wednesday before, but it took the show a whole week to knock him off. I was just in time to catch the Doc choking on the whipped cream.

As Dr. Parker gasped his final breath, which he milked for a full eight-and-a-half minutes, and the camera did a close-up on the half-eaten cream puff, I began to think. That's the one thing about soaps—they make your own problems seem small compared to things like poisoned pastry. Anyway, I began to think that maybe my mother was right. Maybe I was exaggerating the problem with number eight just a little.

What did Bobbi Weston know? She didn't have that many boyfriends. And Kate and Brenda hadn't been all that upset over what Bobbi said in gym class. Kate thought for sure that we'd be matched with someone we would like.

I began thinking about the assembly that morning. I already knew who I liked. Kevin. Kevin McEvoy. If only the computer would match me with him. I knew if that ever happened, I'd just die. So would Bobbi Weston. Kevin was definitely what she called "neat, cute and mature."

Kevin and me. Why not, I thought. The computer could match us. We had things in common. And we were even already friends. Sort of. He always talked to me and Kate in English class. And he didn't talk to very many girls. Kevin even told me that he thought I was really good as Winnifred in the school play. Besides, why would he have told me that unless he secretly liked me?

Sure, we could be matched, I thought. It could happen. Unless—unless Kevin answered questions like number eight the way Bobbi said the boys would. If he liked what Bobbi said all boys liked, then I'd need a miracle. (Fat chance for that. All the really good miracles stopped about three hundred years ago.) The story of my life: Born too late.

Still, praying for a modern miracle couldn't hurt. My grandmother says you have to have faith no matter what. And this situation definitely came under the heading of no matter what. Just the kind of stuff St. Anthony was in charge of: Lost Causes and Hopeless Situations. I lay back on the couch, closed my eyes, and started to pray. I figured my body would give him a real challenge.

After about fifteen minutes of steady Hail Marys, I opened my eyes and stared down at my chest. So far, there were no signs of any miraculous happenings. I decided St. Anthony needed more time and figured I'd try to reach him again in another hour. In the meantime, I thought I'd catch up on my TV watching. Some game show was on, and a fat lady had just won a trash compacter. She was jumping up and down and screaming. How could anyone get so excited over garbage?

Even a cartoon had to be better than that. I went over to the set to change the channel, and as I got closer to the bookcase, I noticed something shiny on the third shelf. It was a ring I had lost about two weeks before. Well, the day wasn't a total loss. Between boobs, boys and Bobbi, at least something good had happened.

As I picked up the ring and slipped it on my finger, I noticed a thick blue book on the shelf. Its cover had all kinds of crazy signs and symbols written on the front, and across the top it read, *Guide Your Life With the Stars*.

It was an astrology book someone had given Jeannie for her birthday last year. I flipped through the pages and couldn't understand why my sister never used it. It looked pretty interesting. There were a lot of photographs of famous people and events in history, with drawings of zodiac signs like lions and bulls. The book even had chapters that told what signs got along with other signs, and who should fall in love with who, and . . .

Astrology.

That was it!

My prayers were answered. St. Anthony worked faster than I expected. It wasn't exactly what I prayed for, I thought, looking down at my chest; but if it could help me get matched with Kevin, the idea had to be a pretty good runner-up.

All I had to do was let the stars guide the computer. Simple. Brilliant. And, thanks to St. Anthony, divine. As I looked through the book, I decided to study what the stars said Kevin liked and didn't like, then answer my questionnaire just the way he would.

Kate told us in gym that the computer matched people on the basis of what they had in common. With my plan, Kevin's and my answers would be so similar, the computer would have no choice but to make me his dream date. This idea was really foolproof. And I didn't need a body like Raquel Welch or Bobbi Weston either.

But what I did need was Kevin's birthdate. The only way to know what sign he was, was to know when he was born. I dropped the book on the floor. Oh, terrific, I thought. I had no idea when Kevin was born. And I'd probably need another miracle to find out.

That was it, I thought. The end. I plopped back down on the couch and was about to let loose with another therapy scream, when I noticed a cardboard box of pictures on the coffee table. My mother was making a collage out of old photographs of everyone in the family. I didn't like the idea too much when she started the project. After all, I didn't want nonfamily members seeing me as a bald, naked baby. But that was before I saw the picture of me in my pink bathing suit. Before I remembered.

When I was in the third grade, Kevin had a birthday party and invited almost everybody in class, including Brenda, Kate and me. I remembered, because the party was outdoors like a picnic, and it was so hot, everyone went swimming. Me too. That's where the pink bathing suit came in.

O.K., St. Anthony, I thought, getting off the couch. Heaven came through again.

I picked up the book and thumbed to the table of contents. The party was near the end of the summer, because I remembered it seemed we were back in school not long after that. I figured that meant Kevin's birthday had to be around the middle of August, and according to the book, that made Kevin a Leo.

Outwitting the computer was going to be easier than I thought. The very first paragraph in the chapter describing Leos said they got along very well with Sagittarians. I looked that up, too. That included people born in late November like me. I had a feeling that this was going to be cake. Definitely cake.

I sprawled out on the floor, propped my chin under my fists, and began to concentrate on Leos. I read that they were fiery and majestic . . . born leaders. A sign that produced more than its share of American presidents. That book really knew what it was talking about: after all, Kevin was our class president. It also said Leos were dramatic, outgoing, independent and strong, yet sensitive.

Kevin and I had more in common than I had even thought. I was certainly dramatic. My mother was always telling me that. And I was sensitive too. I knew I cried better than anyone in the whole state. Maybe even the country. Nobody's face gets blotchier than mine when I've been crying.

But strong and independent. I wasn't sure if I was really that independent. But then I thought, oh, what the heck. I could fake it. I could act just like the kind of girl that was perfect for Kevin. I knew I could do it. After all, acting was in my blood. I didn't get five curtain calls in the play for nothing.

I sat up and closed the book. My mind was made up. Not only was I going to answer the computer sheet like a Leo. I was going to be a Leo. I decided that in school the next day, I would act really dramatic. Well, more dramatic than usual anyway. More "Leo" dramatic. That would give Kevin some hints on how perfect I was for him; maybe even remind him of the things he really liked. So when the inevitable results came on Monday morning, he would be doubly ecstatic.

Besides, I figured, no sense letting my acting ability go to waste. I could act very outgoing and sensitive, and dramatic—well, just like Rosalind Russell or Bette Davis. Even Katharine Hepburn. I had seen enough of all of their old movies to act just the way they did.

Acting. Yeah, why not act like a Leo, I thought, leaning up against the cushion on the couch.

It couldn't hurt. And it might make sure Kevin answered his questionnaire like the Leo he was. Remind him, as I said, of his basic nature. Then with me matching his Leo answers, the match was sure to be a cinch. Like I said, I had a feeling this was going to be cake. Definitely cake.

Chapter 4

LEO IN THE
SEVENTH HOUSE

 ❧ ❧

The detailed plans for my acting strategy were temporarily delayed. I was called for K.P. Duty by the Italian General. That's what my father has called my mother ever since his diet began. As I marched into the kitchen, she was slicing cucumbers for salad.

Not again I thought when I saw the meat on the counter. Steak, salad and cottage cheese. The Moretti Menu of the Month. And the seventh time in eight days for that cottage cheese. Ugh.

"Ma-a-a, can't we have potatoes just this once?" I whined opening the silverware drawer and picking up the forks and knives. Was it any wonder I was so underdeveloped?

My pitiful cry of hunger got to her quicker than I had expected. She said Jeannie and I could have french fries *if* I peeled the potatoes. I told her that I'd do anything to escape those curds.

I put on an apron (it makes me feel more domestic), and figured I'd plan my Kevin acting strategy as I scraped. I grabbed a peeler and tried to think of some good scenes I could act out in school the next day.

There were plenty of Roz and Bette ones for outgoing and dramatic. I had already thought of *His Girl Friday*. That I knew would be easy to act out since I talked fast naturally. And of course there was *Auntie Mame* and Bette's *Dangerous*. But I wasn't having much luck thinking of scenes for strong and independent. They were tough.

"It shouldn't be too much longer," I heard my mother tell me as I peeled a second potato. "Daddy should be finished with his diet in a week or so, and then we can get back to eating a little more normally."

My mother was making it very difficult to concentrate on being strong and independent. Especially "strong" when she kept talking about food. My stomach was grumbling. I was beginning to weaken.

"I'll even make some of your favorites. How about that?"

"Yeah, good, Ma," I said trying to get back to my plan and remember all the old movies I had ever seen.

"Let's see . . . well, ziti of course. And polenta, cavatelli, well all my Italian dishes. Oh, and I know what you've always liked. What about southern fried chicken? Toni? Did you hear me? I said, what about southern fried chicken?"

Southern fried chicken.

Yeah, southern, I thought, still scraping. Too bad I couldn't act like that southern character Bette Davis played in *Cotton in the Cabin*, I thought. Her southern drawl drove a guy wild. But I knew I couldn't walk up to Kevin in school and say, "I'd love to kiss ya, but I just washed my hair." I thought that might be just a bit too much. Too bad, too, because that southern drawl idea was really . . .

"That's it!"

"What's it? You mean the chicken? Toni?"

Yeah. A southern drawl, I thought. Strong and independent. It was perfect. I could act just like Scarlett O'Hara. I practically knew all of her lines by heart already. I must have seen *Gone With the Wind* at least nine times. That was my favorite Clark Gable movie of all time.

Scarlett O'Hara. Of course. I knew that was my answer to strong and independent. Best of all, men could never resist a willful southern belle. And if it could work on Rhett, it could work on Kevin.

I had loads of scenes to use, too. Strong and independent was right up Scarlett's alley. One really good scene was when she came back to Tara after the Yankees burned Atlanta. She was tired and depressed. Hunger gnawed at her stomach. She was so starved that she even picked up a dirty old turnip, couldn't help herself and . . .

"Toni!" my mother said as I bit into the raw potato I was peeling, the way Scarlett bit into the turnip. "What in the world do you think you're . . ."

I spit a mouthful of potato into the sink, fell down on the kitchen tile, looked up and cried, "As God is my witness, nobody is going to lick me. Not even Bobbi Weston. As God is my witness, I'm never going to be hungry again."

Boy, I was wishing Kevin was there to see that. He would have been better than my mother.

"Toni! What are you doing? Toni! For heaven's sake, if you're that hungry, all right, you don't have to stay on your father's diet. You don't have to resort to all these dramatics."

"Oh, Fiddle-de-dee, Mammy," I said standing up and fanning my apron. "Now, don't y'all worry about me. I'm jess fussin' over that Valentine's Dance, that's all. But I jess won't think about it now. I'll think about it later," I said, walking back to the counter and picking up the potato peeler. "I'll think about it tomorrow. . . . After all, to-morrow is another day."

"Well, tomorrow may be another day, Tallulah,

but today get going with those potatoes."

I told you my mother has no sense of the dramatic.

But I didn't really care. Kevin was the one I wanted to impress. I went back to peeling and thinking about tomorrow.

That was all I thought about the rest of my peeling, all through dinner, and later when I was getting ready for bed. "Tomorrow is another day." "The" day, I thought. The day when I put all my plans into actions.

I finished brushing my teeth and was about to leave the bathroom, when I thought I'd use the john one more time before going to sleep. Just to make sure. If there's one thing I hate, it's getting up in the middle of the night to go to the bathroom.

As usual, there was no more toilet tissue. I had to improvise with Kleenex. That was Jeannie for you. She never replaces the roll when she uses it up. I wish we didn't have to share a bathroom. As it was, I was lucky when I got to use this one at all. My sister is in there night and day. Always getting ready for Rich. Boy, I never knew before she started going with him that you had to shower so much to have a boyfriend. But I guessed I'd know for myself soon enough.

I stood over the sink and washed my hands, then

looked in the mirror and laughed. My mother probably thought I was crazy when I rehearsed my Scarlett.

"Well, fiddle-de-dee," I said flipping off the bathroom light and walking into my bedroom. I didn't care what anybody thought, as long as I was matched with Kevin.

The clock radio on the nightstand said 11:35, but I really didn't need it to tell me what time it was. I could hear the TV in my parent's room. "The Tonight Show" was on, and Johnny Carson was doing his monologue. I couldn't hear everything he was saying, but I could tell it was funny because my father was laughing.

As I went to shut my door and turn out the light, I noticed the astrology book on my dresser. I had taken it upstairs with the rest of my books when I did my homework after dinner, but I never had a chance to read any more of it.

In fact, I had almost forgotten about it, trying to remember all those old movies. I almost panicked. That book probably still had a lot of stuff I needed to know about Leos. Information that I absolutely had to have for my plan to work. I should know all the likes and dislikes of Leos. It wasn't just the stars from Hollywood that were going to help me get matched with Kevin.

"Toni? Are you still up?" my mother called. "It's

almost twelve o'clock. Turn out your light and go to sleep or you won't be able to wake up for school tomorrow."

I think my mother has mind radar or something, when I start thinking about staying up late.

"O.K., Ma," I said hearing Ed McMahon laugh at one of Johnny's jokes. "I'm turning out the light right now."

Which I did. I didn't lie. I just turned it back on after I closed the door. Then I put a pillow against the crack at the bottom so nobody would see any light coming from the other side.

It was a pretty good trick if I do say so myself. Sneaky, actually, but essential. I try not to be sneaky if it isn't necessary, but this was necessary. It was the only way I could read the astrology book. Even though my mother wears glasses for reading and seeing close, her eyes are great for picking up light. Especially my bedroom light when I'm supposed to be asleep.

I carried the book back to my bed and sat down crosslegged on the quilt. Flipping through the pages, I came to the chapter on Leos and then started to read and memorize everything and anything that would help me answer the questionnaire like Kevin.

The more I read, the more I knew my plan was absolutely foolproof. The book was great. If it wasn't for all of that astrology information, I would never have known that Kevin had a temper or liked parties, all sorts of stuff. The book was really a godsend. Or rather, a saint-send. St. Anthony really knew what he was doing up there.

I felt like reprising a chorus of my show stopper from *Once Upon a Mattress*. I just knew that after Monday when we received our computer matching results, I was going to live "Happily, Happily, Happy Ever After."

I would have chanced a few bars too, if I hadn't seen that it was way past twelve. If my mother had any idea that I was still awake, she would have killed me. She usually laughs when I'm being overly dramatic, but I didn't think she'd go for an encore performance after midnight. She's very big on going to sleep at a "decent" hour.

I was going to play it safe and turn out the light, but then I saw the chapter on natal charts. That was something that was supposed to tell you all about yourself. Even your future. I thought maybe it could tell me if I was going to be a rich and famous actress; or better, it might say who my future husband would be. What were a few more minutes where the love of my life was concerned? I stayed up.

I'm not the best person in the world when it comes to math and calculations. I'm even worse when I can't even keep my eyes open. But, despite droopy eyelids that needed to be propped open with toothpicks (well, just about), I finally figured out that a chart was divided into twelve parts called houses.

Each house represented some area of life, like career, family, marriage, things like that. Every house was ruled by an astrological sign in the zodiac, and the book explained that depending upon when and where you were born, certain planets were placed in these houses, which then influenced and guided your life.

There were lots of examples. If a bad planet, which is Saturn, ruled the money house, that could make you stingy or poor. If Jupiter, a good planet, ruled that house, then you could be rich. Luckily, the book was for beginners, because if it had been any more complicated, I would have ended up with a screaming Excedrin Headache number twenty-five.

But it was worth it.

It was worth Excedrin Headaches number twenty-six, twenty-seven, and twenty-eight. Because it was all there. In black and white. My natal chart said I had Jupiter in Leo. My house of love. Leo was in my seventh house. According to Jeannie's book, Kevin and I were destined to be matched.

I knew it. I knew it.

I couldn't wait to tell Kate and Brenda and I would have phoned them right away, if it hadn't been past midnight. Their mothers were big on going to sleep at decent hours, too. The Mother's Manual again.

I was going to have to wait until tomorrow to tell them about Kevin and me. Kevin and me. It had a ring to it. Like Romeo and Juliet, or better yet, Rhett and Scarlett.

I looked up at the *Gone With the Wind* poster above my bed. Clark Gable was holding Vivien Leigh in his arms, staring into her eyes, sweeping her off her feet, about to kiss her . . . and in a little over one week that would be me and Kevin. I felt it in my bones.

It was in the stars.

I just hoped the computer was into astrology, and Kevin knew himself as well as I knew him.

Chapter 5

ROZ, VIV, BETTE AND ME

❧ ❦

"Toni Moretti, what the heck were you doing in there?" Kate asked grabbing my arm as we left class. "You were talking a mile a minute. I couldn't even understand you. And why did you keep calling me 'Darling'?"

"I told you in homeroom this morning, remember?" I said walking into the cafeteria for study hall. "I'm acting like a Leo. I was doing my 'outgoing' personality. You know, like Rosalind Russell. She always talked fast and called everyone 'Darling' in *Auntie Mame*."

"Well, how the heck is anyone supposed to know that?" she asked as we looked for an empty table. "Who is Rosalind Russell anyway? And what's an Auntie Mame?"

"What's an Auntie Mame? Kate, you know. Remember at my pajama party when we all stayed up to watch that movie on the Late, Late

Show? Well, that's her."

"Oh, yeah! Hey, Toni, you imitated her pretty good. But I still don't get it. Why?"

Brenda walked over and put her books down on the table as I explained about Roz and Mame and how all of that was going to affect Kevin.

"All this acting still doesn't make sense to me," said Kate opening her notebook. "You're using astrology, why do you have to act like Rosalind Russell and Barbara Stanward?"

"Stanwyck, Barbara Stanwyck," I said taking the questionnaire from my pocketbook. "Just never mind about the acting. I have my reasons. I'm covering all bases. I'm leaving nothing to chance. Nothing."

"Well, it sounds good to me," said Brenda wiping her glasses with a tissue. "Especially the St. Anthony part. Boy, you Catholics are lucky. I wish I had a saint helping me with the matching. I guess you and I will just have to rely on the computer, huh, Kate? . . . Kate?"

"What? Oh, right," she answered a bit distracted.

"Hey, let's get started and answer these things," I said looking over my shoulder at the clock on the wall. "If we don't hurry, none of us will be matched, St. Anthony or not."

I looked over my sheet and thought that so far, plan B was working fine. Even if Kate didn't understand. I was sure Kevin had noticed my acting. He definitely noticed my Rosalind Russell and Scarlett O'Hara. In fact he'd looked at me in history class as if he couldn't believe his eyes. I knew that southern drawl would get to him. I thought maybe I would try a little Bette Davis on him in English class. But first, it was on to my brilliant plan A, and letting the stars guide that big old IBM.

I found a pencil with a point and started answering the questions under the category called "general information." This wasn't exactly studying, but the three of us pretended we were doing our homework, so we got away with it. Besides, our table was so far back in the cafeteria, the teacher on study hall duty would never be able to catch us.

General information was easy. The questions had to do with birthday, age, color of hair and eyes. The questionnaire gave choices, so all I had to do was blacken the right square. It sort of reminded me of the multiple choice tests Mr. Hargrove gave in Science class. Only this was more fun, and here I knew positively that I had all the correct answers. I hadn't stayed up half the night memorizing that astrology book for nothing.

The questionnaire also asked how much you weighed and your height. I guess that was to make sure some tall girl wasn't matched with a short boy. The computer probably figured they wouldn't be able to slow dance together.

Of course, there was Bobbi Weston's number eight. 'General physical description.' She was right. I did have to check "petite" to describe myself. But, I figured it didn't really matter. Kevin and I were so astrologically alike, he wouldn't even care about my little you-know-whats.

After we filled in all the squares in the first category, the three of us switched questionnaires to compare answers. It was weird. I mean really weird. Kate's almost looked like mine. We both answered 'brown' for hair and eye color. Our answer for the question on weight was almost the same, too. Only, Kate wrote eighty-eight pounds, three more than I weighed. The one real difference between us was our birthdays. Kate was born in October, and I was born in November.

Brenda laughed when she saw that Kate and I were so much alike; maybe the computer would match us with each other, she told us.

That wasn't funny.

Kate was one of my best friends; well, all three of us had been ever since the first grade; but I didn't want Kate Donnelly for a dream date. I wasn't going to blow all my acting, research and prayers on her no matter how long we had known each other.

I took back my questionnaire, crossed out

"Toni," and spelled my full name "Antonia." I didn't want the computer to think I was a boy. That kind of machinery does foul up sometimes, and where Kevin was concerned, I didn't want to take any unnecessary chances.

"Gee, Toni," said Brenda looking over the rest of the questions, "Do you think your astrology idea could work for me and, uh, Mr. Simmons?"

"Brenda," said Kate looking up from her sheet, "forget about Mr. Simmons. He's too old. He's a teacher. Besides, Toni's plan is only good when you use it for boys in school—like Kevin."

"Yeah, like Kevin," I sighed chewing on my pencil eraser. "Isn't he great? And cute too, don't you think?"

Brenda shook her head. "And popular. Remember how many votes he got when he ran for class president? And he's the kicker on the football team, don't forget that. I bet all the girls will just die when you're matched with him, Toni."

"Do you think so?" I whispered. "What do you think, Kate?"

"Yeah, sure . . . but Toni, well, I don't know about Brenda, but I'm still kind of surprised about your liking Kevin so much in the first place. You never told us before."

I rummaged through my bag for another pencil. "I know. I wasn't sure myself until yesterday's assembly. That really clinched it for me. But I think I've liked Kevin ever since, well, ever since Halloween. Kate, remember when you and I met him trick-or-treating and he asked us to go house to house with him?"

"Wow. Since October?" said Brenda forgetting how quiet the cafeteria was. "Well, anyway," she continued, lowering her voice, "I think it's just great. And that plan of yours is perfect. Don't you think, Kate?"

"Hmmm? . . . Right. Perfect. Hey, let's finish these things, O.K.?" she said. We only had fifteen minutes left in study hall.

We all went back to answering the questionnaires, and I looked over the section where you picked what you wanted your dream date to look like. Naturally, I checked everything that described Kevin. Brown eyes, brown hair, average height and build. (Bobbi's good old number eight.)

It made me wonder what Kevin was checking on his sheet. I hoped he didn't like blonde hair.

After that section, came the one titled, "Your General Attitudes." That's where my astrology research went to work.

"Let's see now," I said looking at the questions from twenty to thirty. "Number twenty: I consider my personality to be (a) outgoing (b) shy (c) average. . . . That one is definitely 'outgoing.' The book said Leos are outgoing. That's what Kevin is, so that's what I am," I said to Kate and Brenda.

"Well, how about twenty-three? How would Kevin answer that? Listen," Kate began to read, "Would you (a) never cheat (b) sneak some answers from a friend (c) make a cheat sheet?"

"Well, the astrology book said that Leos are very honest, so that means Kevin would never cheat."

I blackened the square next to (a), and then went on to the other questions. Twenty-five asked if you liked parties, being alone or just being with one close friend. I figured that that one had to be (a) too, liking parties. The book had said Leos really enjoyed being the life of the party. If that was Kevin, then that was me.

"Boy, this one is tough," said Brenda tapping her pencil on the table. "How are you going to answer twenty-six?"

That one was a little difficult. But nothing my research couldn't handle. It asked, "If you didn't get what you wanted, would you (a) make the best of it (b) complain (c) sulk (d) become angry."

"It has to be (d), Bren," I finally answered. "Leos have bad tempers."

"I don't know if that's how Kevin would answer, Toni," said Kate, looking at the other choices. "We've know Kevin since grammar school, and I don't remember his ever getting angry or even sulking. Do you think Kevin would really lose his temper?"

I checked (d) anyway. I was going strictly by the book. I was sure that that was what Kevin would answer. He was a Leo. He had to check (d). So I had to check (d).

I do value Kate's opinion, but after all, she didn't know as much as I did about Kevin. Or Leos. I had done all the research. I was practically an expert on Kevin's likes and dislikes. And the more answers Kevin and I had in common, the more reasons the computer would have to match us for the Valentine's Dance.

I finished answering the last question at the same time Kate blackened in the square next to number thirty. "Let's all compare answers one more time before we have to leave," she suggested putting down her pencil. "Just for fun."

The bell rang just as I handed Brenda back her sheet and Kate gave me mine. As the three of us walked through the cafeteria doors, Brenda told us she was going to drop her questionnaire in the box in the lobby during passing.

"I think I'll wait until later," said Kate. "I want to go over mine one more time. I'll probably stop by the lobby after class."

"Me too," I said scuffing my feet on the waxed floor as we both headed for the stairwell. "I want to give mine one more quick once-over."

"O.K.," said Brenda walking toward the lobby. "See you two later. And, hey Toni, good luck with your plan B acting."

My acting.

I had almost forgotten about that. I climbed the stairs behind Kate and wondered what I should try on Kevin next. Maybe fun-loving or dramatic. Or both. I thought I might as well go for broke with all the Leo characteristics I could think of. It was Friday, and I wanted to leave Kevin with a lasting impression for the weekend.

Kate and I walked into room 302, and as I sat down, it came to me. I decided to start off with a little fun-loving routine a la Katharine Hepburn from *Bringing Up Baby*. Then I'd mix in some dramatic Bette Davis from *Dangerous*. (She won an Oscar for that one way back in the '30s. It was an oldie, but goodie.) Bette flirted like crazy through the entire movie. That should clinch it, I thought.

After my Roz, Scarlett, and now Bette, I knew Kevin wouldn't be able to resist me. I thought he might even rig his own answers to make sure he was matched with me.

The final passing bell sounded, and Mrs. Berg-
man entered the room to begin class. I turned to
Kevin and smiled a *Dangerous* smile.

Move over, Bette, I thought to myself.

Here comes Moretti.

Chapter 6

T. G. I. M?

❧ ❦

Sister Carmella-Marie's bifocals would have cracked if she could have seen me that weekend. Me, Toni Moretti, actually praying the beads off my rosaries. And I wasn't even in church. I'll bet I set a Guinness World Record for religious multiplication. Those little purple beads were probably flattened for eternity. So were my knee caps. But it was worth it. I wanted to be absolutely sure of getting matched with Kevin when we got our computer results that Monday. With God on my side, plus my acting and astrology research, I knew I couldn't miss.

I sat on the bed and pulled my socks up as close to my knees as possible. My knees looked weird. Being holy was taking an unhealthy toll on my body. But as I said, it was worth it. I wasn't going to take any chances where Kevin was concerned.

Not that I didn't have faith in my astrology plan and acting ability. I just thought a few extra Our Fathers to God and St. Anthony couldn't hurt. I even lit four candles after Sunday's Mass. And—I made an offering of $3.82. (I would have given more, but that was all the money I had left over from my birthday present from my grandmother.)

The money wasn't a bribe or anything. (I don't think you could bribe God.) I thought of it more like added insurance. A sort of double indemnity policy with the stars and saints.

I pulled my bedspread over my Kliban quilt and pillow (the closest thing I'd ever get to a pet cat if my father had his way), and pounded out the lumps.

T.G.I.M. Thank God It's Monday, I thought. I knew I couldn't wait another day for those computer results.

Usually I hated getting up on Mondays. But that morning, I was up, dressed and downstairs for breakfast all before 7:30. A mini-miracle according to my mother, who said she hadn't seen me up that early since the Christmas when I was six.

I guess that's what love does to you. Love for a Leo that is. Actually, being in love with Kevin was getting pretty tiring. I hadn't had a good night's sleep since last Thursday when the whole computer idea started. I had thought about Kevin so much over the weekend, I couldn't even sleep late on Saturday morning. Me not sleeping late! In my house, Toni not sleeping late on Saturday was unheard of. And as unbelievable as it sounds, I had so much nervous energy, I actually cleaned my room! I even dusted. I didn't cheat by dusting around stuff either. I really dusted.

My mother was still giving me one of her "I don't believe this is my daughter" looks as I took a pitcher of grapefruit juice from the refrigerator.

"That clock does say seven-thirty, doesn't it Toni?" she said sipping her tea as I grabbed a glass from the cabinet above the dishwasher.

I poured the juice and took a gooey coconut doughnut from the box on the counter.

"Yup, it's me. I guess even I can get up early once in a while."

"Mmmmm . . . so I see," she said adjusting the glasses on the bridge of her nose. "It's just that I see it so infrequently. What has gotten into you all of a sudden with all the early rising and room cleaning?"

Why do mothers think the world begins and ends with not sleeping till noon and having a clean room?

I sat down next to her and said not to get too excited, because down deep I was still sloppy and lazy I thought. That my cleaning urges were probably only temporary. (Like temporary insanity.) It was all caused by nervous energy about the dance.

"Well, if that's true, I wish you had a dance every week," my mother said buttering a piece of toast. "I didn't know a dance could stir up energy for housework."

I didn't know it either. But then, all those psychiatrists on TV said you had to work at being in love. And this must be what they meant.

I gulped a last swallow of grapefruit juice and winced. That stuff was wicked. I couldn't wait for my father to lose his twenty pounds and have my mother go back to buying good, old-fashioned orange juice.

"What? Toni Moretti up and practically ready for school all before eight?" My sister said coming into the kitchen. "And on a Monday yet. There must be something wrong with her, Mom. She's gotta be sick."

She tied the belt on her robe and walked over to the sink to pour some water into the tea kettle.

"Quick Ma," she said, "where's the thermometer? The kid's got to have a fever."

"Funny, Jeannie, real funny," I said finishing a bite of coco-goo. "For your information, 'the kid' is up because I'm glad it's Monday. Today is the day we get the computer matching results for the Valentine's Dance."

"What dance?" asked my father coming into the kitchen with the morning paper. He sat down and turned to the sports page, giving me a funny look. "Why are you up so early? You aren't sick, are you?"

Naturally my sister thought that was hysterical. You would have thought my father was Steve Martin or something the way she laughed. What a warped sense of humor. Can't a kid get up early without the whole family making a federal case out of it?

"Toni isn't ill. She's just excited about the school dance," my mother explained as she brought my father his bowl of Special K and poured his coffee. He said he'd skip the grapefruit juice. Smart move.

"A dance? Is that right?" he said before the three of us caught him sneaking sugar for his cereal.

"Getting back to Toni," he said innocently, trying to change the subject. "Who are you going with? Do we know him, Rosemary?" he asked my mother as he opened his newspaper again and hid behind the page. (Trying to steal a piece of toast no doubt. For a cop, he sure leaves a lot of clues to his crimes.)

"Toni doesn't even know who the boy is, Daddy," said Jeannie, pouring boiling water into a tea cup. "The dance is a computer dance. All the kids filled out those questionnaire things, you know." She babbled on as she dunked her tea bag. "Toni told us about it a couple of nights ago at dinner."

"*I* can tell Daddy all about the dance, Jeannie. And I can tell him *who* I'm going with too."

My mother looked up from a section of the newspaper my father had given her and said, "Toni, I thought you told me you were getting the results this morning?"

"Yeah, I know." I got up from the table and walked over to the sink to rinse out my glass. "But that's really for everyone else. I know who I'm going to be matched with already, because I filled out my questionnaire scientifically. This morning in homeroom just makes everything official."

"What are you talking about?" Jeannie said biting into a chocolate doughnut.

"I'm talking about science. You know, subconscious implants, the stars, research," I said standing by the counter. "I used this terrific plan on how to get matched with exactly the boy I really like. I outwitted the computer. I used one of your books, too, and my acting ability, of course. It's foolproof. Brenda, Kate—everyone—thinks so."

"Oh brother! I was right about you in the first place. You are sick," Jeannie said licking her fingers. "Outwitting a computer . . . acting ability . . . and what book are you talking about? I don't have any books on computers."

"I know," I said walking back to the table. "I used your astrology book. The one that was in the family room, *Guide Your Life With the Stars*. I used the horoscopes and zodiac signs—and get this —I 'acted' out all the characteristics of my perfect match. I acted like Bette Davis and Rosalind Russell—even Vivien Leigh as Scarlett O'Hara. How 'bout that y'all?"

I pulled out a chair and sat down next to her and said, "I just hope the computer is into astrology. Well, really it doesn't matter, I guess. The stars in my natal chart say I'm destined to be matched with this boy no matter what, because my sign is Sagittarius and he's Leo."

"Oh, I can't believe this!" Jeannie said laughing and almost choking on her tea. "Toni, tell me you're not that dumb," she coughed. "Bette Davis, Scarlett O'Hara, and astrology. Astrology! I can't believe this. Do you honestly think you're going to be matched with some boy because of that junk?"

"It isn't junk," I said.

"It is too junk."

"O.K. Jeannie, that's enough," my mother said taking off her glasses. "Let's just wait and see. Although Toni, why you went through all of this is beyond me. Why didn't you just fill out the questionnaire like everyone else? Why all this business with Scarlett O'Hara and astrology and . . ."

"Ma-a-a."

How could she forget what I had told her about Bobbi Weston and number eight? Without this plan, my chances of having a perfect match—any match—were the pits.

"See," Jeannie said interrupting. "Your own mother thinks this whole thing is stupid, too."

"Now, Jeannie, I didn't say that. Toni could still be matched with this boy."

"Well, don't count on it," my sister said finishing her doughnut. "Toni, how could you be so dumb? Sagittarius . . . Leo."

My father put down the paper he was hiding behind and said, "Well, I for one would like to know more about this boy, Leo."

"No Daddy," I said. "His *name* isn't Leo. His *sign* is Leo. His name is Kevin."

Of course, Jeannie thought that was the funniest thing she had ever heard in her life.

"Do you see how ridiculous this thing is?" she said getting up from her chair.

Then she started to go on and on about how dumb I was to believe in astrology. Nobody really believes in astrology she said. Just because my sister goes to college, she thinks she knows everything. But this is where I had her. I told her that obviously she never read any magazines or she would know that a lot of movie stars believe in astrology.

"Oh, please. Not that movie star nonsense again," she said.

"O.K., forget movie stars. There were people in history who believed in it, too. Famous people, like . . . Marco Polo and Ben Franklin and

Thomas Jefferson and all sorts of people. So there. And you think you're such a great history major."

"Well, here's a news flash for you, Toni," she said standing by the dishwasher. "Hitler believed in astrology too. Need I say more?"

Why couldn't I have been an only child?

"Now, Jeannie, leave your sister alone," my father said getting up from the table as he glanced at his watch. "You just do what you want to, Toni," he said giving me a kiss on the forehead. "We all have to learn by our own mistakes."

Boy, that was a vote of confidence for you.

"Well, I'd love to hear more about this dumb plan, but I've got to get dressed," Jeannie said, following my father into the hallway as he left for work. "Hey, Miss Sagittarius," she called climbing the stairs, "I'll drive you to school if you want. Rich is picking me up. We have an early class this morning."

"No thanks. Brenda's mother is picking Kate and me up today."

Thank goodness. I didn't think I could stand those two mush faces that early in the morning. What Rich saw in her was beyond me.

I looked at the clock above the refrigerator. It was a little past 8:15. Mrs. Erdman would be at the house in about five minutes. I gathered my school books and put my arm through the sleeve of my coat while my mother reminded me to bundle up. The weather report on the radio that morning had said the temperature was only twenty-two degrees.

"And wear your scarf," she said as I tucked my hair under a knitted hat. "I found it this morning in the broom closet, of all places. I don't know for the life of me how you lose these things. I put it on the bannister for you, so now don't forget it," she called as I walked into the hallway. "It's cold this morning."

I glanced out the window just as Brenda's mother turned their station wagon into our driveway. As she honked the horn, I grabbed my scarf and was about to run out the door when I heard Jeannie. She was talking on the upstairs phone to Rich and laughing about my plan. What a warped sense of humor!

Well, just wait until after homeroom, I thought walking out to the car.

We'd just see who had the last laugh.

Chapter 7

ET TU, KATE?

❧ ❦

The wind was blowing so hard, I was barely able to hear Brenda as the three of us ran up the sidewalk to the school entrance.

"What did you say?" I asked.

I opened the door and watched Brenda's glasses fog up as we stepped into the warm building.

"Listen Toni," she said wiping the inside of her lenses with her gloved fingers. "I told you, forget about your sister. What does she know anyway? My older brother is just like that. Ever since he started shaving, he thinks he's a real know-it-all."

We walked through the corridor to our hall lockers as Kate added further moral support.

They were right. I was right. My plan was perfect. Foolproof. The acting, astrology—and St. Anthony. How could I miss with him? When you pray all weekend to a patron saint of lost causes and make an offering of $3.82, he's not going to let you down.

We stood by our lockers and dialed the combinations. Mine was stuck as usual and I had to dial it four times before it yanked open.

"Darn that stupid thing," I said kicking the door then tossing my hat on the top shelf. "Why does it have to act up this morning? First my sister, now this."

"C'mon, forget it," Kate said as I picked up the books for my morning classes from the locker floor.

"Yeah, let's get to homeroom early." Brenda said as the three of us rushed down the hall. "Maybe Miss Vernon will hand out the computer results before the bell rings."

But Miss Vernon wasn't going to hand them out early. She wasn't even in class yet. Most of the kids were already there though. A big difference from the mornings when we're issued our report cards. I guess everyone was as excited about those computer results as we were.

We sat down at our desks just as the bell rang. Miss Vernon still wasn't in class, and it was already past 8:40.

"Where is she?" I said looking at the clock above the blackboard. "Don't tell me she's late today? Or sick? Oh, great! She won't be in at all, and the substitute probably won't know anything about the computer dance or the—"

"Shhhhhhsh," Kate said as Miss Vernon walked into the room carrying a stack of thin white envelopes.

"There they are," whispered Brenda as we watched the teacher place them on the upper right hand corner of her desk. "This is it! This is really it."

But when was "it" really going to happen? We only had fifteen minutes for homeroom. You would have thought Miss Vernon would hand out the computer results right away. Especially since she was late and had already wasted two minutes.

But she didn't.

First she took attendance. That wasted about three more minutes. Then she got into some dumb conversation with a kid who forgot his note from home explaining why he wasn't in school last week. There she was yakking about school policy and wasting precious minutes while my future love life was sitting right on the corner of her desk.

Finally when we only had about five minutes of homeroom left and my palms were totally wringing wet, she started handing them out.

"Alan Boardman . . . Gary Channing . . . Michael Franklin . . ."

Alphabetical order! And boys first no less! We'd probably run out of time before she got to the M's in girls.

". . . Robert Sawyer . . . Brian Warner . . . Frannie Ashton . . ."

Finally. The girls.

"Cathy Chayko . . . Kate Donnelly . . . Jennifer Ellington . . . Brenda Erdman . . ."

Brenda practically leaped from her chair to the front of the room when she heard her name. I had to nudge Kate, though. She's always so calm. Although how she could be calm about these computer results, I'll never know.

I hadn't heard any "ughs" yet as people opened their envelopes. The boys seemed satisfied. There was a lot of shoulder punching. A couple of girls whose names were called before Kate's and Brenda's even said "Wow" when they read their results. I guess the computer did O.K. Brenda and Kate came back to their desks just as Miss Vernon called,

"Ellen Kosup . . . Antonia Moretti . . ."

Kate said she and Brenda would wait to open their envelopes until I got back to my seat with mine. As Miss Vernon handed me my computer result, I heard a couple of kids wonder aloud why I used the name Antonia instead of Toni, the way I usually do. That's because they didn't know how careful I had been with my plan. After finding out in study hall how much Kate's questionnaire looked like mine, I didn't want the computer to think I was a boy because I used the name Toni. I didn't take any chances where Kevin was concerned.

"So c'mon, let's open 'em," said Brenda tearing off the top of her envelope as I sat down. "I don't know about you two, but I can't wait any more."

Kate and I watched her face as she read the little slip of paper.

"Oh, wow," she said smiling.

"Sexy Simmons?" said Kate.

"I think better," said Brenda. "Timothy John Stevenson. You know, T.J, the boy in my art class."

"Is he nice?" asked Kate.

"Nice? He's a hunk!" she said looking for a comb in her bag. "How do I look? I have art first period. My hair is probably a mess, right? I think I'll take off my glasses and . . ."

"You next Kate—alphabetical order," I said as Brenda concentrated on T.J. Even though I think I was more excited than Kate (boy was she calm), I wanted to be polite. After all, I already knew who my match was.

"O.K., O.K.," she said tearing the corner off the envelope and poking her finger through the hole and down the side.

"So . . . So . . . ?" said Brenda putting away her comb as we both watched Kate read the results. "Who's your dream date, Kate?"

We couldn't understand why she wasn't answering. I thought she was even beginning to look a little sick.

Poor Kate. I hoped she wasn't matched with someone really awful. But it couldn't be that bad.

"Let me see," said Brenda taking the paper from Kate's hand.

"Well?" I said after Brenda read the results. "Well, who is it? Come on you two, it can't be that bad. No one is . . ."

"Toni—it's, it's . . . Kevin," said Kate. "I'm matched with Kevin."

Kevin? Kevin McEvoy? My Kevin McEvoy?

That had to be impossible. Impossible. I looked at the piece of paper that Brenda handed me. It wasn't impossible. It was true. There it was in black and white: Kate Donnelly—dream date, Kevin McEvoy. A phone number was right next to an address.

I couldn't believe this. What had happened to my research? And my rosaries? What had happened to St. Anthony?

I don't remember if I cried or not. I'm surprised I didn't throw up. Not that I didn't feel like it. I think it was only sheer determination not to be totally humiliated twice in less than thirty seconds that stopped me.

I just couldn't believe this was happening to me. My perfect plan. My foolproof plan. A fiasco.

What had I done wrong?

Then I got scared and went into a cold sweat. Suppose God thought I was trying to bribe St. Anthony with that $3.82? I'd probably be damned to a life of hell, and this was just the beginning.

Kate said she was sorry or something, and Brenda kept telling me there must have been a mistake with the computer. Everything will be straightened out, someone kept saying. The bell rang, and we walked to first class together. I must have walked, but don't ask me how. My feet felt like lead. I don't remember how I walked into history class. All I know is that it was history, because Brenda wasn't there. Brenda wasn't there, but someone else was.

Kevin.

There we were. The three of us. Sitting in history class together. Kate, Kevin and me. Just four desks apart.

Luckily, there was still a few minutes before the bell rang. I was sure Kate would tell Kevin there had been some mistake and that she couldn't go to the dance with him. Then everything would be straightened out, and I could go to the dance with Kevin.

Those few minutes seemed like hours, and when the final bell rang and Mr. Prescott closed the door, Kate still hadn't said anything to Kevin. I couldn't figure out what she was waiting for. The situation was embarrassing enough, without dragging it out further.

As the teacher started to write the reading assignment on the blackboard, I opened my history book to chapter twenty-one and glanced toward Kate. She was talking to Kevin. Finally. Explaining the whole mix-up. I knew she would straighten the whole thing out. I felt a little more relaxed and began to read. That was before I happened to look up and see Kate whisper something to him and smile. Then I heard Kevin whisper something back, and I saw Kate shake her head "yes."

I felt my face getting hot. My lower lip started to quiver, and I knew my eyes were teary. This wasn't happening. It wasn't. I just couldn't believe Kate was saying she'd go to the dance with him. She couldn't be. Kevin was mine. She knew the stars said he was my perfect match. I was the one who had done all the research. All the acting. All the praying. I had the flattened knees to prove it. I was the one who liked Kevin. She couldn't do this to me.

I covered my mouth with my hand, trying to force back a quiver. I couldn't burst out crying in front of everybody. I had to act as if nothing was wrong or end up even more humiliated with a tearstained, blotchy face. Talk about Oscar-winning performances.

I was trying to inconspicuously blink away some tears when a teacher knocked at our door and motioned for Mr. Prescott. He hadn't been in the hallway for two seconds when Kate was talking to Kevin again. They were talking a little louder, and I heard Kevin tell her he was glad they were going to the dance together. And Kate didn't say one word about me! I couldn't believe it. Not one word. What she did say was that she couldn't believe they were matched. I bet.

She could believe it, all right. So she didn't know who she liked, eh? So I had to nudge her to pick up her computer result, eh? I was slowly beginning to see how this whole thing had happened. What a conniver she was. What a sneak. I had been stabbed in the back. Stabbed just like Brutus stabbed Caesar. They were supposed to have been best friends too, weren't they?

I should have seen this coming. How could I have been so blind? The entire thing was right out of one of my favorite movies. And I must have seen *All About Eve* at least six times. I was sucked into that sappy, sweet, best friend routine of Kate's just the way Bette Davis was by Anne Baxter's Eve. Eve wanted Bette's boyfriend so she tried to be just like her—only better—so she could steal him away.

I watched Kate as Mr. Prescott came back into the room. Now she was writing notes! Some best friend. She had probably used all my astrology answers. All my research. Sure. She had watched me fill in my questionnaire right in study hall. And it was her idea to compare answers. She must have copied them. Every single one. No wonder she was so calm in homeroom. She knew the whole time that she was the one who would be matched with Kevin. She knew the whole time that she would have just one more thing in common with Kevin than me, because they're both Irish. She's even a bigot! What a sneak!

And to think I'd felt sorry for her. I'd actually thought she looked sick. Sick! Guilty is more like it. Best friend. Hah!

The class ended as the two of them were passing their umpteenth note. I gathered my books and headed for the doorway. It would have relieved my feelings to tear Kate's hair out, but I restrained myself. I shouldn't have. As I walked past their desks, I heard Kevin tell Kate that she was just about the only girl in school that he liked.

Key word being 'just about.' I was probably the 'just about.' And I would have been 'the' girl he liked if it hadn't been for that rat Kate Donnelly. There she was, my supposed best friend in the whole world, actually saying nothing to him about me. Nothing! Zero! Zip!

I didn't know what to do first. Scream. Be sick. Or kill her. Unfortunately, I couldn't do any of them. I didn't have time.

I hurried into the hall and was heading for second period when I met Brenda. She tried not to act too excited about T.J. Stevenson. I guess she could tell I needed sympathy. At least I still had one best friend in this world.

"So what happened with Kevin?" she asked as we walked through the noisy, crowded corridor. "Did everything get straightened out?"

"Straightened out? Let's just say that our 'dear friend' Kate is in for a bumpy night," I said, quoting a line that Bette Davis said in *All About Eve*.

"Huh?" said Brenda turning the corner. "What did you say?"

"Oh, nothing. Forget it."

"Well then, what about the dance?" Brenda said as some boy bumped into her, making her almost drop a book.

"Dance? Forget the dance, too," I said. "If I can't go with Kevin, I don't want to go at all. And our 'friend' Kate Donnelly is going with him. The big sneak. You know, Brenda, she stole him from me. Can you believe it?"

Brenda tried to tell me that maybe there was some misunderstanding. Sure. The only misunderstanding was that I had misunderstood when I thought Kate was my friend.

As we walked into our math class, Brenda said, "So forget about Kate and Kevin. Who were you matched with, anyway?"

"I don't know," I said sitting down. "Who cares? I didn't even look."

"Didn't look? You have to at least look, Toni. C'mon, let's see," she said, finding my computer result envelope at the bottom of my notebook. I was hoping I had lost the thing. "Maybe you're matched with someone better than Kevin," she went on, tearing the corner of the envelope.

I just gave her a look that said, "Better than Kevin?" Dream on.

"Well, why not?" Brenda said. "I didn't think there could be anybody better than Mr. Simmons, but I was matched with T.J., and believe me, Toni, he's really nice. You know, I bet you're matched with someone really nice, too."

Brenda was trying so hard to be a good friend (and goodness knows I needed one), I didn't have the heart to tell her that there was no comparison between Mr. Simmons and my Kevin. No matter how much of a hunk she thought he was.

"So?" I finally said watching her read my results. "Who is it? Creepy Carney, right?"

"Of course not," she said as more kids entered the class and sat down. "Actually, this is pretty good."

"Come on, Brenda," I said taking the slip of paper from her. "Don't make this better than it really is. I can take it. Let me read it . . . Jack

Campbell?" I said, reading the name. "I never heard of him. Who the heck is Jack Campbell?"

"Oh, you know," she whispered after the final passing bell rang, and the class started. "He's an eighth grader. He's on the football team with Kevin. The kids all call him 'Soup.' Get it? Soup Campbell?"

I got it all right.

Well, now I knew the day was complete. A know-it-all sister, an unreliable saint, a rotten friend and a dream date called chicken noodle.

Chapter 8

REPLAY:
"AAAAAAAA
aaaaaahhhhhhhhhh. . . "

≥ ≤

"AAAAAaaaaaaaaahhhhhhhhhhh," I screamed
coming through the front door and plopping down
on the living room couch.

I was tense again. And depressed. Really depressed. Olivia de Havilland, *Snake Pit* depressed.
And if you've ever seen that old movie, you'd
know what I was talking about.

"AAAaaaaaahhhhhhhhhhhhhh."

I took the scarf around my neck and pretended
to strangle myself. Isadora Duncan had all the luck.
Choked to death when her silk scarf got caught in
the wheel of her convertible. That ended her acting and dancing quick enough. Did I know anyone
with a 1920s roadster?

What a day. The whole day was absolutely
pathetic. That rotten Kate Donnelly, I said over
and over again. I never wanted to see her face as

long as I lived. What kind of friend would steal astrology answers and pretend not to even like Kevin, when the whole time she wanted him for herself?

No wonder she wasn't upset when that boy from the other school came down with the flu and couldn't take her to the Christmas Dance. She didn't want to go with him anyway. She'd always wanted Kevin. And she stole my answers to get him. How greedy could she get? One boy wasn't enough for her. Nooooo, she had to have the boy I liked, too.

I was betrayed. Betrayed by my best friend, and sold down the river with some guy named Soup.

"AAAAAAaaaaaaaaaahhhhhhhhh," I screamed again taking off my jacket and tossing it on the floor with my hat and scarf.

The pits. It was the pits. My life was the P.I.T.S. And that St. Anthony. He was some help. Instead of getting me out of a hopeless situation, he'd gotten me into one!

"You hear that up there, St. Anthony?" I yelled staring at the ceiling. "Why didn't you at least warn me about Kate? What's the world coming to when you can't even rely on a saint?"

What was I doing, I thought. I couldn't afford to be yelling at a saint at a time like this. If this whole mess was because God thought I was bribing St. Anthony with that $3.82, I was done for.

"AAAAAaaaaaahhhhhhh," I screamed kicking my shoes into the air.

Bribing a saint . . . there weren't enough beads on a rosary for God to forgive that one. I began to worry that if He was mad enough, maybe He wouldn't even let me live through the night.

I didn't know how I'd lived through that day. I'd thought I would go crazy listening to everyone else in school talk about their wonderful dream dates for the Valentine's Dance.

And of course, there was Kate and Kevin. Kate and Kevin. They sounded like the Bobbsey Twins. What they acted like was Siamese Twins, the way they walked to every class together. Kevin even saved her a place in the lunch line. Ugh. Disgusting. Absolutely disgusting. If I hadn't wanted to watch that little conniver every minute, I would have gone to the school nurse to see if I could go home sick. It wouldn't have taken much more of "Kate and Kevin" for me to throw up all over the clinic.

"AAAAAaaaaaaahhhhhhhhhh."

"Toni? Screaming again?" my mother said rushing into the living room wearing nothing but a slip. Not exactly her usual attire, but right then I couldn't be concerned with incidentals.

"What did I tell you last week about that screaming? And pick up your things before your father comes home," she said hurrying past me holding a dress in front of her.

"Ma . . . Ma!" I said sitting up. She was just the person I wanted to talk to. After the day I just had, I needed some motherly comfort.

"Ma," I said following her through the living room. "Ma," I said following her into the dining room. "Ma," I said following her into the kitchen and finally the laundry room.

"Ma? Wait a minute. Are you listening to me? Ma? This is it, Mom. The end. My life is over. Over. Ma? MOTHER."

"Oh, Toni I didn't see you. Did you pick up those things as I asked? Oh, and Honey, while you're here, do me a favor and plug in the iron, hmm?" She said putting the dress she had been carrying on the ironing board.

The way my luck had been going, I wouldn't have put money on it, but I could have bet she hadn't heard a word I'd said. Not one word.

"Ma-a-a," I whined, plugging in the cord. "Mom, listen to me. My entire life is ruined. Totally ruined. I've lost the only boyfriend I've ever wanted. My best friend—make that supposed best friend—is a rat, and to make matters worse, God could be planning to send me straight to hell. I think I committed a sin, Ma. A biggie. And after today, He might be giving me a sneak preview of my condemned hereafter. Ma?"

"Hmmmm? Oh, Toni, before I forget, you and

Jeannie will have to make yourselves dinner to-night," she said moving the iron back and forth over the skirt of the dress. "Daddy and I are going into the city to see a play. Uncle Joe got some un-expected tickets, so Daddy and I and Uncle Joe and Aunt Dolores are all going. For dinner, too. Isn't that nice? I can't believe I'm actually getting your father to see something besides a basketball game. And, oh," she said looking at the clock above the washing machine. "Look at the time. I only have fifteen minutes to dress. We have to catch a four-thirty train."

Not a word. She didn't hear one word. I'm go-ing to hell, and she isn't even listening.

"Ma . . ."

"What? Toni, please. I can't talk now. Tell me later," she said slipping the dress off the ironing board. "Daddy will be home in a couple of min-utes, and I'm not even ready. Unplug that iron for me, O.K.?" she called over her shoulder as she ran up the back hall stairs.

This was unbelievable. Any other time, my mother practically gave me the third degree about what happened in school. She had to know EVERYTHING. The one day I WANTED to tell her something and . . .

"Ma," I called running up the stairs behind her and into the bedroom. "Let me just tell you about this. This is so horrible—so despicable—wait until you hear this," I said, falling on the bed and watching her put on her make-up.

As she applied a purplish lipstick, I told her about the computer results and the "betrayal."

"Kate matched with Kevin?" she said standing up from her dressing table chair and slipping into her dress.

"Right. Do you believe it?"

My mother motioned for me to zip her up in the back and said, "Kevin. Isn't that the boy you wanted to be matched with?"

"Mom, that's the whole point."

Sometimes I wonder if talking to my mother is worth the trouble.

"Kate stole Kevin from me. She used all of my astrology answers and who knows what else. The big sneak."

"Toni! Stop that. Kate is one of your best friends. Now you know better than that. I've always thought she was such a sweet girl. Now, where are my shoes," she mumbled looking through her closet.

"Don't you see, Mom? That sweetness—it's an act. All an act. Like Eve in *All About Eve*."

"Oh, Toni, really! Don't be so dramatic." She laughed.

Laughing. I was ripped off in the boyfriend department, and my own mother was laughing.

"There must be some other explanation," she said walking past me and kissing my forehead.

Finally, I thought. Some comfort. Some affection.

"I hope I don't freeze my toes off in these shoes," she said putting on a pair of suede sandals. "What do you think?"

Toes? Shoes? That affection was sure short-lived. That's when I knew it was no use. I would get nowhere talking to my mother. I felt a scream coming on.

"Rosemary? Are you ready?" called my father opening the front door.

A-ha. My father. Now, he was the one I had to talk to, I thought. He would probably get into an uproar when I told him what Kate had done to me. Policemen were big on crime and injustice. I thought maybe I could even have my father arrest her.

"Rosemary," he said to my mother as we both came down the stairs. "We only have about seven minutes to catch the train. Joe and Dolores are waiting in the car."

"Daddy—wait till I tell . . ."

"I thought you'd be ready by now," he said to my mother as she put on her coat. "Oh, hi, Toni. Rosemary, do you see the time? We'll never make it with all this rush hour traffic. I knew we—"

"O.K., I'm ready Lou," my mother said kissing him as she looked at herself one more time in the hall mirror.

A kiss *and* a Lou? She only calls him that when she's real mushy, or at Christmas after she's had a couple of eggnogs. Usually she calls him "Dad," which always sounds pretty dumb to me since he's not her father. She probably expected this to be a big night. Well, that was that. I knew I didn't have a chance of getting through to either of them now. A scream was definitely coming on.

"Now Toni," my mother said as they were walking out the door. "Remember to lock the front door before you go to sleep. And there's money for you and Jeannie on the kitchen counter if you want to buy something for supper."

"Rosemary . . ."

"Pizza? Or Chinese? Well, whatever."

"Rosemary," my father kept saying tugging at her sleeve.

"We won't be too late. Be good. And hang up your coat," she reminded me before my father closed the door.

Who said, "There's no place like home"?

I went back to the living room couch to lie down. It was obvious I wasn't going to get any family sympathy. The only thing left for me to do was to plot some revenge against my former "friend" and Kevin. No, not Kevin, I decided.

I'd spare him, and save him for myself later. But Kate . . . for Kate Donnelly, I'd show no mercy.

Why should I? The little schemer. No wonder she'd kept asking to compare answers on the questionnaire. And then she hadn't wanted to hand hers in with Brenda after study hall. She said she'd wait. Yeah, wait to change all of her answers to the ones I had so she'd be matched with Kevin.

I got up from the couch and walked into the family room to turn on the TV. I thought maybe watching a soap opera would give me an inspiration for some kind of juicy revenge. Nothing as drastic as a poison cream puff, but close. I figured if I was going to hell, I might as well enjoy myself before I got there.

But the soap opera idea didn't work. It only made me more depressed. It was not a revenge day at Mercy General. It was more like a love day. Every scene was kiss, kiss, kiss.

That I didn't need. I didn't need anything to remind me of love and romance. Thinking that Kate could get her very first kiss from Kevin made me just . . .

"AAAaaaaaaaahhhhhhhhhhhhhh."

How depressing can life get?

"Bombed out today, huh?" said Jeannie walking into the room.

"When did you get home?" I asked not bothering to answer her question.

"Oh, a minute ago, I guess," she said sitting on the arm of the plaid chair. "Just in time to hear your familiar screams. Your acting and astrology didn't work, huh?"

Believe me, when I get to Broadway, she's one sister who'll have to beg me for free tickets.

"So what?" Jeannie continued. "Big deal. There'll be other dances. Listen, if you're matched with somebody you don't like, just don't go to the dance, that's all," she said popping her chewing gum.

"Yeah, well, I bet Mommy will make me."

"I bet she will too, Bette Davis." Jeannie laughed falling onto the chair.

That girl definitely has a warped sense of humor.

"Hey, what do you want for supper? I saw the note Mommy left on the table," she said changing the subject. "No diet tonight. Do you want hamburgers? Rich can drive us."

"Why don't you two go alone and bring something back for me."

I wasn't in the mood to watch those two mush faces eating. My stomach couldn't take it on top of everything else.

Luckily she liked my idea. I knew she would. She doesn't need too much of an excuse to be alone with Rich. She said she was going to call him and then leave in about ten minutes.

Good. I'd be left alone with my misery. I stared at the TV, not paying any attention to it, and wondered why all of this had happened to me. I had used my acting, astrology, and God. Where had I gone wrong? Maybe I should have checked out my biorhythms.

I was in the middle of another scream when the phone rang. Obviously, Jeannie wasn't going to answer it. If she knows it isn't Rich, she doesn't bother. Otherwise, she practically kills everybody and everything in her path to answer it first.

It was already on the fifth ring, so I figured I was the only one to pick it up. I hoped it wasn't Aunt Anne. She'd probably talk to me for the rest of my life, and I wasn't up to discussing school, church, or my cute cousin Connie.

"Hello?" I said.

"Hi. May I speak to Antonia Moretti?" asked the voice on the other end.

"This is Antonia, I mean, Toni Moretti."

"Hi, Toni. This is Jack Campbell."

Soup.

Just what I didn't need on an empty stomach.

Chapter 9

I AM NOT . . . AM I?

❦ ❦

"What a week. Thank God it's Thursday."

"Well, I told you," Jeannie said loading the dishwasher with dinner dishes, "Girls do funny things where boys are concerned."

"Funny isn't the word," I said wiping the table. "It's disgusting what Kate did to me. Absolutely disgusting. I mean, really Jeannie, can you believe it? Can you? One of my best friends. I've known her since the first grade, and look what she does to me. Steals my boyfriend. And not just any boyfriend, but probably the love of my life."

"Love of your life, come on, Toni. Kevin wasn't really your boyfriend."

"That's just a formality. Kate knew that I liked him. Same thing."

"Well, I still can't believe Kate would do something like that," Jeannie said sprinkling the soap detergent into the dispenser.

"Exactly, exactly. That's why she pulled it off. I never even suspected that she could be so low that she'd steal my astrology answers."

"Toni, you don't really believe that dumb astrology stuff had anything to do with this, do you?" she said turning on the switch.

"Of course I do. It had everything to do with it," I said sitting down at the kitchen table. "How do you think Kate ended up with Kevin and me with someone named Soup?"

"Oh yeah, how is Soup?"

"No jokes about his name? Thanks. Although I don't know how you resisted. It's so dumb sounding and—well, anyway, he's O.K., I guess. His ears stick out, but he's O.K. But he's not Kevin."

"Toni, why don't you try to be a good sport about this and accept the fact that Kate is going to the dance with Kevin?" my sister said taking a glass from the cabinet and pouring herself a glass of milk. "That poor girl has been calling here all week. You could at least talk to her and hear her side of the situation."

"What? Talk to her? Talk to Kate Donnelly? Never. I'll die before I'll ever talk to her again."

"Oh, that's cute, real cute," she said biting into a cookie. "But then, didn't I say that girls do funny things where boys are concerned?"

"And what is that supposed to mean? You know, Jeannie," I said taking a sip from her glass, "just because you go to college and take one, I repeat, *one* course in psychology—that doesn't make you some kind of doctor. You don't know every-thing."

"You're right. I don't know everything. But I know when you're jealous. Anybody can see that."

Jealous? Me? My sister was crazy, I thought.

"Get out of here," I said. "I am not. Jealous of Kate Donnelly? I wouldn't waste my time. I'm not jealous, I'm just mad."

"Oh, sure. Just mad. You haven't talked to your best friend in nearly a week. You've blamed her for everything you could possibly think of. Blown this entire thing out of proportion. Sure. That's just your everyday 'mad.' Je-a-lous! You are jea—"

That was it. I had had it with her.

"Hey, Miss Know-it-all, when I want your opinion, I'll ask for it. And I'm not jealous," I said running upstairs to my bedroom.

I fell across my bed and stared at the poster above the headboard. Rhett was still holding Scar-lett. Still staring into her eyes. Still about to kiss her.

I felt the closest I'd ever get to anything like that was right then. Just looking. While Kate, yeah while Kate . . .

I pounded my pillow and wanted to scream. My best friend. How could she have done that to me? She never even said she liked Kevin. Never. Not even once. Not even a hint. So why would she intentionally try to be matched with Kevin when I wanted him?

I sat up. The only logical answer, I thought, was to spite me. Some girls were like that. Bobbi Weston for one. She used to be friends with a lot of girls until she started going out with boys. Then she began acting like a real big shot and was snotty to the other girls and . . . so, I thought, Kate believed that she was the new Bobbi Weston? Dating Kevin, one of the cutest, most popular boys in school, she probably thought she was too good for me and Brenda.

But then, as far as I could tell, she was still friendly with Brenda. She was only rotten to me. Of course, I knew that would only be until she decided she liked T.J., and tried to steal him away too.

I didn't know what to think. Kate couldn't be like that, I told myself. Could she?

I looked back up at the poster of Rhett and Scarlett.

Kate could, would, and did when the boy was Kevin.

I wanted to scream.

All I wanted in my whole life was to go to a dance with Kevin. And what did I get? Soup. From Kevin to Campbell Soup. It wasn't fair. And that wasn't being jealous. No matter what Jeannie thought. Anybody would feel like that if it happened to them. I wasn't jealous of Kate. I just hated her.

No, I thought. I didn't hate her. Did I? I began to wonder if I could really hate her. I looked over at the photograph on my dresser. It was a picture of Kate, Brenda and me taken two summers ago when Kate's parents had a house down at the shore. We had our arms around each other and were holding a sign that read, "The Three Musketeers." Three Musketeers. How corny could you get? Kid stuff. Who needed it?

Who needed someone to walk to school with, or talk on the phone to, or swap lunches with when your mother gave you liverwurst?

I began to think about what Jeannie told me in the kitchen. Was I really jealous? Was I blowing this whole thing out of proportion? Was Kevin really worth not being friends with Kate?

"Yes!" I said aloud throwing the picture on the floor and turning over on the bed. Kate and Kevin. Kate and Kevin. Kate and Kevin. Everywhere I looked.

And I couldn't believe that she actually had the nerve to try to talk to me. "Explain." Sure. Calling me at home every night, well, that was just too much. What did she think I was?

I walked over to the dressing table and looked at myself in the mirror. All I wanted at that moment was to get through Friday. One more day I kept thinking. Then the dance and Kevin—even Soup—would be over with. Then things could get back to normal.

Normal.

That word sounded like a foreign language to me. Would anything ever be normal again I wondered.

It couldn't be normal. Not without Brenda, Kate and me being friends, I thought picking up the photograph that I had thrown on the floor.

I didn't know what to think. Maybe . . . maybe Kate being matched with Kevin was just a coincidence. Maybe I had jumped to the wrong conclusion. Maybe I was just a little jealous, like Jeannie said. I was sometimes jealous of her and Rich. I knew for certain I was a little jealous of Bobbi. No, a lot jealous, I thought again looking down at my chest.

I didn't really mean to be jealous. It was just that I knew nobody would ever like me the way I was. I knew that Kevin wouldn't. The computer was my only chance to have a boyfriend like everyone else and . . .

I wondered if I should try to talk to Kate before the dance. Maybe straighten things out. Then again, I wasn't sure. Suppose she was guilty, the way I had thought all along?

But then I thought what Jeannie said.

I didn't know what to do.

"Toni? Toni?" my mother called knocking on my door. "There's a phone call for you. It's Kate."

My mother opened the door. "Honey, did you hear me? I said Kate is on the phone."

I got off the bed and put the photograph face down on the dresser.

"Tell her I'm not home."

Chapter 10

SO LONG,
ST. ANTHONY

So, here I am.

Is this the worst night of my life or what? Like I said before, St. Anthony, where were you when I needed you? Where are you now? Are you still listening?

Hey, I'll even let bygones be bygones. (And after the week I just told you about, I think that's pretty nice of me.) Couldn't you come up with one little semi-miracle?

Well, what's the use? 7:16. Nothing is going to save me, so I better quit stalling and dress. Dress for doom. Doom. Capital D-O-O-M. What a waste of a new outfit. My mother buys me black velvet jeans, a matching vest and a silk blouse, and it's all wasted on somebody named Soup.

Thank you, Kate Donnelly. Former friend. Would you believe she called me two more times last night after I told my mother to say I wasn't home? She must be riddled with guilt. If she had any sense of decency, she wouldn't go to the dance with Kevin at all.

If I had my way, I wouldn't go to this dance either. But noooo. My mother says I have to. I knew she'd make me. Everything will work out fine, she says. Sure. With Soup.

But who wants Soup?

"Toni, are you dressing?"

"Yeah, Mom. Don't worry, I'm going."

"All right. Come downstairs when you're ready. Your date should be here in a few minutes. You don't want to keep Soup waiting."

"Why not? Will Soup get cold?"

"Toni . . ."

"O.K., O.K., I'll be down in a minute."

Geez. I must have the all-time classic case of unsympathetic mother. Father, too. He actually laughed this week when I asked him to arrest Kate. Some police chief! Someone in his own family reports a theft, and he does nothing. And my sister! Forget her. Doesn't anyone care that my social life is over before it even begins? I told you I was ready for the convent.

I wonder what Jeannie's astrology book would say to all of this. Probably give up and die. What else? It's the only answer.

What I want to know is, where did I go wrong? Well, I know partly. St. Anthony turned out to be the most unreliable saint of all time. (I'm going to report him to the Pope, too.) And of course, Kate cheated. But my acting was perfect, so was my astrology research. How could it have gone wrong? That computer must have short-circuited or something.

It had to. There is no other explanation. It's here in black and white, page 183: "Leos and Sagittarians are the perfect match." And I know positively that Kevin is a Leo. I checked that out yesterday with one of his friends. I couldn't have messed up the astrology. Kevin was definitely a Leo, and I answered the questionnaire just the way I was supposed to. I answered just like a . . .

Just like a Leo. I answered like a Leo. A Leo! A Leo! I answered like a Leo, not like a Sagittarian.

What about Leos paired with other Leos? Where is that page? Why do my fingers have to be so sweaty, just when I need them? *A Leo male should not expect to share exactly the same qualities and tendencies as a Leo female. Some rivalry is possible. A relationship between these two can either be marvelous or totally disastrous.*

It's scream time. That's where I made—my mistake. What an idiot. What a complete idiot. I answered those questions all wrong. I answered like Kevin's sign when all I had to do was answer like my own. That's why the computer didn't match me with Kevin. It thought I was a Leo!

But wait a minute. Wait just one minute! Why was Kate matched with Kevin? If her questionnaire looked so much like mine, why was she matched with him?

I may be sick. Suppose Kate is innocent. Suppose there is some other explanation to all of this. Suppose Kate didn't use my answers after all? Maybe the only answers that seemed alike were those physical description ones.

Where's the chapter on Kate's zodiac sign, Libra —people born in October. The first line under the title 'Librans and Leos': *In general, this can be a rewarding partnership.*

I'm going to be sick. It's worse than I thought. The whole chapter is about how well Librans and Leos get along. Paragraphs and paragraphs about how much they have in common. The author could have written an entire book just on them. 'A perfect match!' That computer was more into astrology than I thought, which means that Kate didn't have to use my answers at all. The stars were guiding her and Kevin from the start.

But what about me? Why weren't the stars guiding me? Why didn't someone warn me? At least stop me from making a fool of myself over Kevin? Acting like Rosalind Russell and Bette Davis. The whole school probably thought I was an idiot.

And Kate. Who knows what she thinks of

me. Jeannie was right. I was jealous.

Yes, jealous. And now, because I had to use that dumb astrology book, I'm not even going to the dance with someone who could match me. I'm going with Soup, who should be going with a real Leo.

Oh no! God? . . . St. Anthony? . . . Someone up there? Tell me why I didn't just answer that questionnaire like a Sagittarian? Like me?

I feel like tearing my hair out . . . and believe me, the only thing that's stopping me is knowing my mother would still make me go to the dance, even if I was bald . . . and I don't need any more humiliation.

Well, that's it. It's over. I'm off to the nunnery. Why not? I deserve to be shipped off to some jungle. I ask you, how could I have been so stupid?

I can just imagine what this dance will be like. Everyone will be laughing at me. Making a fool of myself over Kevin. Being so snotty to Kate. They probably all think I deserve to be matched with someone named Soup. And then there's Bobbi Weston. Oh, I can just hear her.

And look at that stupid clock. Already 7:31. Will this miserable night ever end? Where is St. Anthony now? How hopeless does a situation have to be before he shows up?

This situation is worse than Lucille Ball could ever have gotten herself into on "I Love Lucy."

This is worse than the time when William Holden melted her putty nose with a cigarette lighter. This is worse than the time when she got her skirt caught in a bicycle and she missed the boat to Europe. This is worse than the time she was frozen stiff in the basement freezer. This is even worse than . . .

"Toni. Jack is downstairs, are you ready?"

"Yeah, Ma, I'm ready. Come in."

"Well, don't look like you're going to the firing squad, for heaven's sake. Now, come on, Tallulah. We've all had enough of your dramatics all week. Stop acting like this is the end of the world."

"Ma, I'm not being dramatic. This time I'm not exaggerating, honest. Everything is hopeless. You won't believe how hopeless. I've ruined my friendship with Kate, I mean I really ruined it. Finished. The end. Kaput. I know I'll never, ever have a date, not even in my whole life. And— I'm the laughingstock of the whole school. I'll tell you something else, too. I'm not praying to that St. Anthony again. Ever."

"St. Anthony? What does St. Anthony have to do with all of this?"

"Lost causes, Mom. He's the patron saint of lost causes, remember? Only he's lousy at his job. Capital L-O-U-S-Y. I've been praying to him all week. I even spent all the rest of my birthday money in church lighting candles, and what has he done? Nothing. I think I should get a rebate. And how come you're smiling?"

"Oh, am I smiling? I'm sorry, honey."

She was doing it again. Pretending not to smile, when she was really smiling.

"Toni . . . dear . . . St. Anthony is the patron saint of lost things, not lost causes."

"What?"

"Yes, Honey, I thought you knew that. Remember how Grandma always prays to St. Anthony when she loses something or other? No wonder we've been finding those missing things of yours around the house. Your ring, the library book and how about when I found the scarf in the broom closet? Oh, and I forgot to tell you, I found the gold locket that Grandpop gave you last year for Christmas. It was under the chair cushion in the den."

"O.K., O.K., Ma. That's enough. I get the picture, but I don't believe it. On top of everything else, I've been praying to the wrong saint. This is too much. Cover your ears, Mom. I think I'm going to scream."

"Now, calm down. You'll see, everything will work out . . ."

"Fine? I can't believe it. Everything is finished. Oh, Ma, I need help. I mean I really need help. And I don't mean Mark Eden either. Forget boobs, I need help in the brain department."

"Now stop this. You don't need help. Don't be such an actress and just relax. Things will work out. You and Kate will probably talk and make up. You wait and see. You just go to the dance and have a good time."

"But, Ma-a-a."

"No buts."

"Ma? Please? I can't face Kate and Kevin and Brenda . . . and Bobbi. Ma, I can't go to the dance with Soup. Everybody is going to laugh at me. Please Ma, do I have to go?"

"Yes, you have to go. I don't know why you're making all this fuss. Nobody is going to laugh at you. And for heaven's sake, give Soup—Jack—a chance. He seems to be a very nice boy. Even your father likes him. He's talking to him right now."

My father talking to someone named Soup? I better get down there before he starts asking the kid for identification and blood samples.

"Ma, before I prepare for the longest night of my life, wait a minute . . . please . . . for future reference, which I need immediately, who *is* the patron saint of lost causes?"

"Toni? Is that really necessary?"

"Mom. I'm not kidding. Only divine guidance can help me now."

"All right. St. Jude. Now, come on. You don't

want to be late. It's almost a quarter to eight. The dance starts in fifteen minutes."

Only fifteen minutes until the beginning of the end?

I wonder how fast St. Jude is at working miracles.

Chapter 11

TOMORROW
IS ANOTHER DAY

ঙ ʁ

Like my grandmother says in Italian, "*Cu sapa.*"
Who would have thought it? Not me, that's for
sure—at least not the way that evening started:

I could see the illuminated clock on the dash-
board of Soup's father's car, 7:54. Well, I remember thinking, in a couple more minutes, we'd
be at the school, and I would have to live through
the worst night of my entire life. In front of the
whole school no less.

And forget about St. Jude. At least in the in-
stant miracle department. He probably required a
rosary down-payment before he worked on a
hopeless cause. Since I only had time for two quick
Hail Marys before I got downstairs, there was no
miracle waiting. Only Soup.

I thought my parents would have tried to help
me out. But noooooo. My mother actually said,
"What a handsome couple" five times. I counted.

I was surprised my father didn't drag out the Polaroid.

So, the evening was off to a rotten start. I'd known all week that it would be rotten. I had expected it to be rotten. But even I didn't expect it could be that rotten.

Being stuck in Africa with the lepers didn't sound too bad after all. At least as a nun, I wouldn't be worried about boys or fooling around with astrology or ruining friendships. And for sure, I'd know which saint was which. Praying to St. Anthony. How could I have been so dumb?

What a mess. If I hadn't been sitting between Soup and his father, in a compact car yet, I would have let loose with one of my patented screams. But I figured I'd save it until I was back home. I was sure I was going to have plenty of those stored up by the time the night was over.

We drove up to the school just as a few other kids arrived. Luckily, I was able to walk inside without anyone noticing me. So far, so good, I thought. At least group humiliation would wait for a few more minutes.

We hung up our coats on a metal rack in the hall, and after Soup handed in our tickets, we walked into the cafeteria.

It was dark, but I could still see how it was decorated. There were red and white hearts and cupids pasted on the walls, and the tables set up around the dance floor were covered with red tablecloths. There were even white crepe paper streamers strung from the middle of the ceiling to the top edge of the walls. It looked like a big white canopy over the dance floor. My very first dance. This whole thing would have been pretty romantic too, if I was only with . . .

"Hi Toni."

Dark. But not dark enough. Someone still noticed me. Fortunately, it was Brenda and T.J. and not someone like Bobbi Weston.

"This must be Soup, right?" she said squinting at him even though she was standing only a few feet away. "Soup, I mean, Jack Campbell?"

I introduced everyone, and then Soup shook hands with T.J. saying, "It's nice to know you. And, it is Soup. I know that sounds kind of funny, but because of my last name, the guys on the team gave me the nickname. I guess it sort of stuck."

I thought my mother should have been there to hear that. Everything will work out fine? Sure, Ma.

"Yeah, about the team," said T.J. "You guys did O.K. this season. And you, man. Hey, you can really run. Some of those passes you caught were great, too."

"Yes. Really great, Soup," said Brenda.

I gave her a look like, "What are you talking

about?" Brenda didn't know anything more about football than I did. All she knew was to throw confetti every time anybody yelled or screamed. Although I had paid attention when Kevin kicked the ball. But Soup?

"Hey, why don't we all sit down?" said Brenda looking to the rows of round tables. "How about over there?" she suggested, pointing to one in the corner.

Good idea, I thought. It was even darker in the corner. Maybe, if I were lucky, which I knew was wishing the impossible, just maybe I could avoid Kate and Kevin for the night.

We walked over to the table, and as Soup pulled out a chair for me, Brenda mouthed the words, "what a hunk."

A hunk? I'd say that was overdoing it a bit. Soup wasn't bad, but he didn't come close to Kevin. His hair was O.K., if you liked dark brown, practically black. And his ears were still sticking out. I guess Soup had a nice smile, a little devilish or something though. In a way he reminded me of someone, but I just couldn't remember who it was. Anyway, he was athletic looking, like Kevin. His shoulders were wider though, and I think he was taller too. But then, after all, Soup was one year older. But a hunk? Brenda wasn't wearing her glasses. Anybody could look good blurred and in the dark. Even I didn't look bad.

T.J. asked how we liked the decorations, which then prompted Brenda to tell us which cupid she drew and what heart she pasted. And to think I once thought I wanted to go to this dance, I thought. I knew I wouldn't have felt so dejected if I had been sitting next to Kevin. If only I had answered the questionnaire like a Sagittarian instead of a Leo. Well, what was the use. The astrology book said that Kate and Kevin were the perfect match, anyway. I knew I had to accept it. I didn't have to like it, but I figured I had to do my penance.

The band was already playing its fourth song when Brenda began describing in step-by-step detail how she and T.J. had made the papier-maché computer that was on the dance floor. When she came to the chicken wire stage, I sort of turned off my ears and tried to pretend to listen. I couldn't take any more reminders about the computer and how I messed up such a good idea.

I started watching the couples dancing under the canopy. They looked as if they were really having a good time. A scream was definitely coming on.

"Toni?" I heard Soup ask. "Would you like to dance?"

Dance? Me and him in front of everybody? I was about to panic, and then I thought, Oh what the heck. At that point, what did I care what anybody said about me. I had to face total humiliation sooner or later. Besides, I thought, as Soup and I walked on to the dance floor, that would probably be my first and last chance to dance someplace other than the gymnasium and in something other than my ugly green gym suit.

I felt self-conscious at first. I thought everyone was looking at me and laughing. But Soup was such a good dancer, I forgot all about everyone else and just danced. We were pretty good at it too. Better than anyone else actually. We even stayed for two more songs until we got so hot we decided to take a rest.

"Wow, you two were fantastic out there," said Brenda when we reached our seats. "I even put on my glasses for it, see?" she said pointing to them on her face.

I looked over to thank her when I realized who else was sitting at our table. They must have come in when Soup and I were dancing.

"Hi Kate . . . Kevin," I said almost choking on his name.

"Hi Toni," Kate answered.

Silence.

"Oh, excuse me," I said remembering Soup. "Kate, Kevin, I'd like you to meet . . ."

"You don't have to tell me who this guy is, Toni," Kevin said, standing up and shaking hands with Soup. "How's it going?"

I had forgotten that they probably knew each other from the football team. Well, at least Soup and Kevin were friends, I thought. Now, all I had to do was get back to being friends with Kate.

"So . . ." said Brenda as everyone became quiet again.

"So," said Soup. "Hey, I'm thirsty. What about you, Toni? Why don't we guys get some punch for everyone?" he said standing up as the others followed. "And Toni," he whispered in my ear as he bent over, "don't dance with anyone else while I'm gone."

I felt my cheeks get hot and red as the three of them walked across the cafeteria to the refreshment table. Certainly not because of what Soup had whispered. (That was dumb, I think.) It was probably because I was face to face with Kate for the first time since Monday.

The three of us were still quiet. Then, I guess out of desperation, Brenda asked Kate how she liked the Valentine decorations.

"What do you think, Kate?" she asked pointing to the cupids and hearts."

"I'll tell you what I think," I said turning to Kate before she could answer. "I think I'm a big dope. I'm sorry, Kate," I said swallowing hard. "I know that you didn't steal my answers. I shouldn't have said you cheated. I feel awful."

"Me too," said Kate sighing with what I guessed

was relief. "I tried to tell you all week that I was sorry I was matched with Kevin and you weren't but . . ."

"Yeah, I know, I know. But I wouldn't let you."

"Honest, Toni," said Kate talking louder as the band began playing another song. "I never even thought about taking your answers. And I was shocked on Monday when I read those results. I know I should have told you more then, but Kevin started being so nice to me in history class. I don't know. I couldn't help myself."

She didn't have to explain. It was just what the astrology book said. Libra-Leo magic. Those stars just didn't lie. It was true. When I really thought about it, Kate and Kevin did have a lot in common. They were kind of like Ashley and Melanie. Quiet and studious. I started to think that maybe Kevin wasn't my idea of Rhett Butler after all.

"Well, then," said Brenda interrupting my thoughts, "do you two think we can all be friends again?"

"Absolutely," I said, with Kate agreeing. "And hey, let's make a pact. The three of us—no matter how many dances, no matter how many boys, we won't let anything or anybody come between our friendships."

"No more boys," Kate joined in.

"Hold it. Hold it," said Brenda. "Let's not get carried away. I don't know about you two, but there's plenty of me to go around for both of you and a boyfriend!"

We all decided, on second thought, that Brenda's idea sounded better. A lot better.

Well, I for one, was glad that was settled. I knew the evening wouldn't be a complete disaster. Even if Kate did still have Kevin and all I had was Soup.

"So, how are you and uh, Kevin, getting along?" I asked trying to be a good sport. It was still KILLING me though. I guess jealousy dies a slow death.

"Fine, I guess," Kate answered. "You know, Kevin is kind of shy. Quiet. Not really as confident as when he's up on stage as class president. And he doesn't dance. But of course, I'm not much of a dancer either. We do talk. Mostly about school. History mainly. He loves history."

School? History? Kevin talked to a girl about Paul Revere and the Declaration of Independence? At a dance? He was more like Ashley than I thought.

"What about you and Soup?" she said.

"Huh? . . . Oh," I answered still thinking about Kevin and the Revolutionary War, or should I say Civil War, "we really haven't talked much except for a few times at school and on the phone. I guess he's O.K."

"O.K.?" said Brenda taking off her glasses.

"Maybe you should borrow these," she said pretending to hand them to me. "Haven't you been looking at him? I think he looks just like . . ."

"Here we are," interrupted Soup, as he and the others came back with the punch. "I brought back some cookies too, in case anyone was hungry," he said taking the plate off the top of the two cups and placing it on the table.

I was sipping the cherry punch when I looked over to Brenda, who was again mouthing the words, "what a hunk" and pointing to Soup. That time she was wearing her glasses.

Soup was sort of nice. And a good dancer. Maybe Brenda was right, I thought. He was handsome. Well, sort of. He still reminded me of someone. But I just couldn't place where I had seen his face before.

After the punch and cookies, the time went by quicker than I thought it would. Before I knew it, it was almost 11:00, and one of the singers in the band announced that the next number they played would be the last.

Almost everyone in the cafeteria got up from their tables and walked out onto the dance floor. Everybody but Kate and Kevin. They didn't dance one dance all night. (He must have been past World War I by then.)

Soup directed me to the dance floor, and as he put his arm around my waist, I felt a chill down my back. I figured someone must have opened a window or something. That cafeteria was always drafty.

As Soup pulled me towards him, I felt his hair touch the side of my cheek and I shivered again. I was hoping that whoever opened that window, would shut it already. I was getting goose bumps. What I didn't need was to catch pneumonia just when everything was turning out O.K.

It really was O.K. The evening had turned out to be a good one after all, I thought, closing my eyes and dancing. I didn't even care about Kevin anymore. Well, almost. But I did think I was beginning to accept him with Kate. And Soup? Well, believe it or not, I was beginning to like him. I think he liked me too. And I hadn't needed to use St. Jude or Bette Davis or astrology or . . .

I opened my eyes and almost tripped over Soup's feet.

If it wasn't because of St. Jude, or astrology, or my acting, then why did Soup like me? I thought we were totally mismatched. Wasn't Soup supposed to like a girl who was a Leo?

I wasn't a Leo. I wasn't even acting like that sign. I hadn't done any Roz or Bette scenes all night. And I hadn't prayed to St. Jude since those Hail Marys at home.

So then, I thought, how could Soup like me?

Maybe he didn't like me. I began thinking . . . of course he didn't like me. The stars didn't lie. They didn't for Kate and Kevin; wasn't that proof? I was sure that Soup was just trying to be polite and not hurt my feelings. He probably liked someone else and . . .

"OOoooooooohhhhh, excuse me," Bobbi Weston said as she bumped into us. "Well, hello there, Soup. How is everything going?" she said to him motioning to me.

"Fine, Bobbi. Everything is just fine. Hey, see you later, O.K.?" Soup said as we danced away.

He said "see you later"?

"Do you know Bobbie?" I asked.

"Hmmm? Oh, yeah. I dated her a few times."

Dated her a few times? Soup and Bobbi? Soup and Bobbi "The Body" Weston? I knew for sure that Soup was just being polite. I was definitely no competition for Bobbi. Not even a close run-ner-up. Soup must have thought the computer blew a fuse when he found out he was matched with me. The flat-chested Sagittarian.

"I guess you really like her, huh?" I said while the band played an encore.

"Who? Oh, you mean Bobbi? She's O.K."

I knew it. I knew it. I knew he liked her.

"But, there's someone I like better now."

Someone better than Bobbi, I thought? Better

than Bobbi Weston? I didn't know someone like that existed. At least in junior high.

"You know, Toni," Soup was saying as we danced farther away from the other couples on the floor, "to be honest with you, I didn't want to go to this computer dance at all."

Here it comes, I thought. The inevitable. He was letting me down easy. But did he have to do it here?

"Actually, the coaches at school sort of pressured all the guys on the teams. You know, total participation."

Oh no! He HAD to take me. He was forced.

"Well, I'm embarrassed to tell you . . ."

He was embarrassed!

". . . but I didn't answer those questions on the questionnaire truthfully. I didn't answer like myself. In fact, I just answered any old way. That's why," he said holding me tighter, "I'm so surprised that we hit it off."

"What? I mean, me too," I said getting that shiver again. "I—I didn't answer truthfully either."

"What?" said Soup looking into my eyes.

"No, really," I said not knowing if my feet were moving or not. "I—I was trying to use some astrology technique, and I answered all the questions like a Leo even though I'm really a Sagittarian and . . ."

"No kidding?" he laughed. "I guess that computer really knew what it was doing when it came to matching dream dates. We do match each other, don't we?"

My head was spinning so fast, I don't remember if I said "yes" or not. I just wished I could stop shivering. I was getting goose bumps on top of goose bumps. Why didn't someone close that dumb window already?

Oh! Who cared about a few goose bumps?

Soup liked me. Me! Not Bobbi Weston or some other girl, but me.

I couldn't figure out how the computer did it. It was like a miracle. I hadn't even used my Roz or Bette imitations, or any of that dumb astrology either. I wondered if St. Jude had heard those Hail Marys after all?

I looked up at Soup as we danced beneath the canopy. He smiled, and I smiled back. He really was handsome. That dark hair, that wonderful smile! Who did he remind me of? It was driving me crazy. I just knew I had seen that face somewhere before. Was it his ears? Or, I began to wonder . . . if only he had a moustache . . . yes, if Soup only had a moustache he would look just like . . . just like . . .

"So, Toni," Soup said looking into my eyes. "You're into astrology?"

He was holding me closer. I could feel his lips lightly touch my ear when he whispered, "Guess what sign I am."

My head was swimming. My knees were wobbling. I felt like Scarlett O'Hara being swept off her feet.

I looked up at Soup and put my arms tightly around his neck and thought, "Astrology signs?"

Frankly my dear Soup . . . I didn't give a damn.